VIOLENT NIGHTS

This is a work of fiction. Any references to real events, real people, or real places are used fictitiously. Other names, characters, places, and events are products of the author's imagination, and any similarity to actual events or places or persons, living or dead, is purely coincidental.

VIOLENT NIGHTS

Cover by MoorBooksDesign

Illustrations by Marina Baskakova

ryanmhoward.com

ISBN (ebook) 979-8-9856068-1-2

ISBN (paperback) 979-8-9856068-0-5

VIOLENT NIGHTS

A THRILLER

RYAN M. HOWARD

Illustrations by
MARINA BASKAKOVA

Content Warning: This book contains graphic violence and some profane language. Reader discretion is advised.

VIOLENT NIGHTS

What follows happened over two nights during the fall of 1990, in a small town somewhere in America's heartland.

PART I

A COZY KITCHEN

1

THE SECOND NIGHT

7:39 P.M.

Six people crowded around a little kitchen.

"Your son is safe, Mrs. Tippard," the detective said in his softest voice, though it still had some gravel to it. "This tale's got a happy ending."

Julia Tippard, the last guest to arrive, was both smiling and in tears. The detective laid a consoling hand on her back as she pulled a chair and took a seat at the table. Still standing, the detective then turned to Charm, the star of the evening, whose home they were all in. "And we owe that to this young heroine right here," he said.

Charmane "Charm" Wilson, thirteen, shifted in her chair. She shook her head fast, her chin-length hair whipping back and forth as her cheeks turned red behind her freckles. "That's the last thing I feel like. A *hero*." She spat the word out. "I went along with it in the beginning, you know. When it was supposed to be a prank. I feel awful."

Charm wore black pajamas and sported a swollen purple lip. She sat at the small, round wooden table in the center of her family kitchen. It was a cozy kitchen (perhaps too cozy, some of them would later think), the high but narrow walls making the bulky cupboards seem squished together. The clunky wall phone had a cord so long it puddled on the tile floor.

"That boy is alive because of *you*," the detective said.

Charm seemed resentful of the praise, the muscles in her face tightening. "Fine," she replied, her tone curt. "But—"

"Charmane," Julia chirped through tears. She sat across from Charm, coolly dressed in slacks and a floral-patterned blouse. She was indeed crying, but they weren't sad tears. At least not fully. More like happy (or relieved) tears mixed with some sadness too. She still wore a slight smile. "Charmane, it's okay. You're young. I did more than my fair share of being mean when I was young." She sniffed loudly and let out a tight breath. "Now yes, if this had all been some prank or whatever, I'd have been real ticked, I'm sure. But considering the circumstances . . . I forgive you a thousand times over."

Charm's father, Ralph Wilson, sat next to his daughter with his arm across the back of her chair. He planted a kiss on the top of her head. "God, I'm proud of you," he told her. Ralph was a bony man—scrawny, even—but tough-looking; there was a silent challenge in his usual expression, issued to anyone who met his gaze.

Charm was quiet and conceded to the grown-ups, her expression empty.

The detective, a man named Dave Crockson—or just Detective Dave around town—was of middling age, balding. He always had a portfolio under his arm and wore the same faded suit to work every day. Detective Dave was also amiable, easy to get along with, and therefore well-liked.

That was how he perceived himself, at least.

He did, however, have a real talent for closing cases

quickly, which kept his police chief happy. So it would be fair to assume that closing *this* case quickly was what Dave meant to do tonight.

Behind Detective Dave stood a younger officer in a black patrol uniform. Dave introduced his colleague to Charm's father. "Ralph, this is Officer Sherry Merwittle. She just made detective—only one to make the 1990 class, in fact. She's with me to hear the, uh . . ." He broke off and gestured to Charm. "Well, the account of events and such. Your formal statement, Charm."

Officer Sherry stepped forward. Her untamed curly hair stuck out from underneath all sides of her peaked police cap, and she wore on her hip a large silver revolver that gleamed in the kitchen light. She greeted father and daughter with a warm smile. "Mr. Wilson, pleasure. Call me Sherry. And it's *truly* a pleasure to meet you, Charm—"

"You know, with all of what happened last night, I don't see much that's *pleasurable* about any of this, ma'am," Ralph interrupted.

Sherry opened her mouth, closed it, and then nodded before opening it again. "My apologies. You're right. Poor choice of words."

A short silence.

Charm gave Officer Sherry a friendly glance.

Detective Dave cleared his throat. "Ahem, well, uh, we better hop to it. It'll be late soon, and there's a fair amount to cover. May we have a seat, Ralph?"

"Course, Dave." Ralph motioned to the last empty chair at the table with an open, welcoming hand before cocking his head toward Sherry, a stone glare upon his face. "Only got the one seat left, though."

Trying to be cordial, Officer Sherry took a step back and leaned against the kitchen counter, smiling once more. "I can stand, it's not an inconvenience. I like standing—keeps me poised."

Silence again, everyone staring at her. She added, "Poised means ready."

Detective Dave scratched his forehead, looking down and to the side, plainly embarrassed.

Julia also appeared uncomfortable, gazing around the kitchen at nowhere in particular. "I'm sorry, may I please have a glass of water?" she asked the room, but not anyone specific.

The final member of the kitchen was the Wilson family caretaker, a woman named Betts, who, in her eighties, had lived in the family house longer than anyone. She stood almost elusively in one corner with her arms crossed, unmoving, merely observing. Then she gave Julia a brusque nod and flicked a cupboard door open with one long finger. Wearing a cross over her turtleneck and a stern expression on her face, one only needed a single look at Betts to see she was clearly a devout and serious woman—the type that didn't suffer fools gladly, if at all. Inside her cupboard were a dozen glass cups, each hand-painted or engraved with different farm animals. She grasped the nearest one, etched with white rabbits.

While Betts turned on the faucet and filled up the glass, Ralph looked a tad ashamed of himself, grimacing, one hand on the back of his neck.

"Listen," he said to Sherry. "I'm . . . I guess tensions are just a little high with all that's happened. I agree with Dave. This is a happy ending." Ralph tried giving her a smile. It was a good attempt. "I really don't have another chair, though."

Officer Sherry waved away any remaining tension in the air. "And I really don't mind standing."

With the unexpected elephant in the room quickly addressed and resolved, Julia and Detective Dave didn't appear so ill-at-ease anymore. They relaxed their shoulders and resumed polite eye contact.

"On second thought, no worries about the water, ma'am," Julia said with a weak chuckle. "I don't wanna add a glass to your dishwasher."

Betts discreetly rolled her eyes and emptied the glass into the sink. Out the kitchen window in front of her, the sun began to set on their little rustic neighborhood.

It would be dark soon.

2

——————

Detective Dave settled into the last empty chair with a comfy wiggle. He opened his portfolio on the table and produced a pen. "Ralph, we're sorry it took us all day to get over here, man. It's certainly been a process."

Ralph waved away the apology. "I can imagine. Just cover my buy-in at the next poker game, and we're square." He chuckled.

Dave leaned in a little, regarded Charm. "How are you doing, overall?"

Charm's eyes lowered. She shrugged.

Dave tried to be encouraging. "Well, Billy's doing well at home, all things considered. I sat down with him just a little bit ago." He exchanged a quick nod with Julia before looking back at Charm. "Appears both you kids are quite remarkable. Braver than I'd be, that's for darn sure."

"What'd Billy say about everything?" Ralph asked. He glanced at both Detective Dave and Julia before quickly adding, "We're happy to hear he's good, of course."

"He doesn't remember much," Dave said. "Other than

Charm saving his life, that is. He was pretty much unconscious for everything else."

An anguished, involuntary squeak came out of Julia. She reached down and pulled a handkerchief from her purse on the floor, her tears much more on the sad side now. With her head down, she motioned with a hand for them to continue, not wanting to be looked at as she dabbed her eyes and nose.

This triggered Charm's own tear ducts, her brown eyes dewy with moisture, though she held back the breaking of the dam. Instead it was her voice that broke.

"I'm so sorry!" she croaked. "I knew I had to help Billy when the time came, but if I hadn't gone along with the prank in the first place, probably none of this would've happened." A single tear did manage to break through, speeding down a freckled cheek as her gaze dropped back to the table. What she said next was barely above a whisper. "Damn you, Maggie-Lynn. You were supposed to be my best friend. You failed." She shook her head with wide eyes, as though she still couldn't believe what had happened the night before. Ralph held his daughter a little closer as she finished. "I'm just sorry. I'm so sorry."

Julia had cringed upon hearing the name *Maggie-Lynn*, her shoulders still trembling a bit. Eyes shut, she took a deep breath and went into herself for a moment, as though meditating. Nobody said anything, they just waited. Julia went still. When her eyes opened, they were glistening, and she gave Charm a beaming smile. "You're gonna be just fine, sweetheart. You'll come out of this stronger than ever. Got a whole world of people here to support you. All of us."

"Mm-hmm," Detective Dave agreed.

"That's right," Ralph concurred, choking up. He swallowed hard. "We appreciate that, y'all," he said to the room in a hoarse voice. It sounded like he meant it.

There was a brief moment of silent solemnity, everyone respecting the gravity of the recent events.

Once Ralph had his voice under control again, he asked, "Now, Maggie-Lynn and this other girl—the *new* girl—how are their families reacting to what happened?"

Detective Dave hesitated. "Well, not great," he said with a half-laugh. "Pretty devastated, actually. We went to each home and searched their bedrooms today. Strange girls, both of 'em. Suppose that's obvious now. Firstly, Miss Maggie-Lynn McMillan," he nodded to Charm, "your, well . . . now-former best friend, I presume. Her room seemed normal enough. Stuffed animals, buncha clothes. But she had this hidden collection of murder books under her bed. Serial killer biographies—"

"Jesus Christ," Julia said.

"Ahem," Officer Sherry chimed in. "Dave, uh, ongoing investigations . . . aren't we not allowed to talk about them?"

The inner tips of Julia's eyebrows touched the bridge of her nose as she set her sights on Sherry. "I have a right to know everything about the two girls who hurt my son."

Detective Dave softly held up a hand to his colleague. "Sherry, I respect your admiration for the letter of the law, but this is a small town. You know there's a camaraderie in that. I am gonna give them some details." He looked back to Charm, giving Officer Sherry no chance to respond as he continued the interview. "Okay, we'll come back to Maggie-Lynn in a minute. But this other girl, the younger one, Tildra—" He glanced down at his portfolio. "Tildra Smith. Hmm. How long have you known her?"

"I didn't," Charm said. "I spent the summer in the city, visiting my cousins."

"My sister's family," Ralph said. Detective Dave nodded, writing it all down.

"Maggie-Lynn met Tildra during summer school," Charm went on. "Tildra was a year below us, going into seventh grade. She went to a different middle school before, I think. I only met her last night."

Dave bit his lip. "I'm usually ashamed to speak ill of a child," he said. "But this girl Tildra . . . talk about *depraved*. In *her* room we found these journals. Seems she wrote her own made-up death rituals. Instructions on human sacrifice and whatnot, accompanied with illustrations." He sort of bobbed his head here and there. "Very well-drawn, actually."

"She said she wanted to start her own murder cult," Charm revealed. "Tildra."

Julia cringed again, disgusted but also slightly angered, balling both her hands into fists.

Betts, the caretaker, performed the sign of the cross in her corner of the room.

"Disturbing," Ralph said.

"It is," Dave agreed. "Anyhow, Charm. Okay. So, you met Tildra last night. But did you know about Maggie-Lynn's secret collection? Granted, no material by her own hand like the talented Tildra, but serial killer books hidden away just the same. Did you know about that at all?"

Charm nodded immediately, jerking her head up and down like someone who needed to purge themselves of guilt as quickly as possible. "Yes, I did. I mean, I guess it was odd, but I didn't think it was outright bad. A lot of kids at school are into weird stuff. And she was my best friend, she told me everything. She knew it was an unusual hobby, but Magg always thought that kind of stuff was interesting." She looked down and thought for a moment, her brows furrowed. "Like, she said she was appalled by the dark stuff she read but couldn't stop reading it, you know? She said it was fascinating . . . and that's all I thought it was with her. I was wrong."

The kitchen was silent again. A few nodded their heads out of something like respect or understanding, appreciating Charm's candor in unison.

"Fair enough," Detective Dave said while jotting the information down in his portfolio. "You're doing good. That's a real good insight, Charm. After all, it's not like there's anything wrong with reading true crime, is there? No. But why keep it all hidden under the bed? Unless, for some reason, she didn't want her family or anyone to know she was into that stuff."

Charm considered that, then raised her eyebrows and nodded to acknowledge his point.

Meanwhile, Ralph turned in his seat to cough and noticed Officer Sherry staring at him. She quickly glanced away. Ralph's eyes lingered on her a moment, but she pretended not to notice, admiring the ceiling instead.

Dave finished up what he was writing and placed his pen down. He interlocked his fingers and addressed the room but kept his attention on Charm and her father. "Now, the entire force is at the crime scene—all six officers. We're doing the whole shebang. Taking all sorts of, you know, notes and pictures and stuff." He leaned in again toward Charm, bringing back the softer side of his gravelly voice. "You're not in any trouble. You did the right thing. But I gotta say . . . it must've took a lot outta you to do what you did. Are you ready to tell us everything that happened? From beginning to end, as if we were there with you?"

Charm nodded.

Officer Sherry stood up a little straighter and produced her own pen and notepad. She clicked the pen. Ready.

"Okay," Charm said. She gave a big sigh and began. "So I was really excited to see Magg last night after being apart the whole summer. It was just gonna be a sleepover and—"

"One second," Officer Sherry said, taking a half-step forward. "I'm sorry to cut you off, dear, but . . . well, this is kind of awkward." Sherry faltered, nervous to say what needed to be said. Everyone stared at her, waiting for her to continue.

Finally, she did. "Um, but Dave and I actually need to do this part alone with Charm. Could we please have the room?"

Detective Dave looked like that was news to him, his pale face wide-eyed, brows raised.

Julia said, "Excuse me? Why do you think I'm here?" She caught herself. "Don't mistake me, I'm also here to thank Charm, of course, but . . ." She motioned to Charm with one hand but kept her piercing eyes locked on Sherry. "I need to hear it from *her* what happened to *my* son."

Officer Sherry did not falter a second time. "I understand that, Mrs. Tippard. But it's, you know, our procedure. Protocol-type business. Charm will be less prone to withhold details if the interview is private—just so she's fully comfortable."

Detective Dave shifted uncomfortably. The truth was that Dave dreaded socially unpleasant situations and would always bend toward the least-confrontational method of interaction with the community. Dave preferred keeping things smooth. And it had worked well for him over the years—people saw him as easy to put up with, which meant they would naturally and unknowingly drop their guard and cooperate without being too much of a hassle. This enabled him to close out each case rather quickly. Sure, he didn't solve every investigation (not even most of them), but he knew how to *close* them. He knew how to get people to accept what's what and move on, which just happened to be —from Dave's perspective—really what mattered most when it came to serving the public. He would no doubt say Sherry had a lot to learn.

Ralph, however, had no qualms about confrontation. "Why are you still in uniform?" he questioned Officer Sherry. "Why ain't you dressed like a detective?"

"Well, I haven't bought a suit just yet," Sherry said, friendly as could be. "I only made detective this week."

"Exactly." Ralph snapped his fingers and pointed at her. "Which means we all know just as much about being a detective as you. So look, Charm is going to tell Billy's mother what happened last night. That's what all this is really for. You understand? Let's have our *seasoned* detective take the lead on this." He nodded to Dave.

Officer Sherry maintained a polite half-smile. She wasn't embarrassed, she was irritated. Not by Ralph so much—she was used to men like Ralph—but by Dave. As the department's newly-made detective, she actually was meant to be the lead on this, with Dave merely supervising. But since the moment she arrived, meeting up with him outside the little house, Dave had taken the reins, giving Sherry no chance to even introduce herself.

"It's fine, Sherry," Dave told her, his voice soft.

But Sherry didn't hear him. Not really. Instead, she tried again with Ralph, her tone gentle but firm. "These initial interviews do have to be conducted in private with just us law enforcement. Your daughter may withhold information not because she's guilty of anything, but because there just might be something she's uncomfortable saying in front of everybody. Some delicate detail, maybe something embarrassing—any number of things."

Ralph stared at her open-mouthed, his expression plainly declaring that he couldn't care less what some novice who had just made detective had to say.

Charm sat still, staring down at the table.

"I called Dave here as a courtesy," Ralph finally responded. "To help the department with clearing this all up. Any questions y'all have. I could've just as easily hired a damn attorney and done this, you know . . ." he smirked, "through the proper procedure. Protocol and all that."

With that same polite half-smile, Officer Sherry stared back at him for a long moment before nodding her head and conceding the point, appearing deflated. Afterward she raised her gaze, looking off past Ralph's shoulder and noticing Betts, who was motionless in one corner of the kitchen, arms crossed. Sherry's eyes widened a tad, having forgotten the caretaker was there. "And you, ma'am? Do you absolutely need to be present?"

Betts raised her chin at the officer. "Beg pardon?"

Ralph issued a snort of amusement while Betts took three steps forward, stopping right behind Charm and putting her hands on the girl's shoulders. Betts looked at Officer Sherry, then to Detective Dave and Julia.

"Charm's grandmother was my dearest friend growing up," she announced for all to shut up and hear. "As adults, Kansas in the thirties was a hard place, especially in the farmlands. We helped each other through it. But after many years passed, she fell into evil and became unfit to be a parent. So when she gave birth to Charm's mother, I was named godmother and raised her myself." The kitchen had gone dead quiet. Betts continued. "Three decades of real decent memories followed. But ultimately, the Lord needed

Charm's mother more than I did—and shortly after she gave birth to Charm, Jesus called her home, her destiny fulfilled. That's when I named this girl Charmane like her mother wanted and became *her* godmother."

"Grand-godmother," Charm quipped with a faint smile.

"Ma'am, it's quite all right," Detective Dave said to Betts. "Everyone can stay, so long as Charm is comfortable with—"

But Betts wasn't finished. She held up a long finger. "I've had no children from my own womb," she said. "And it hasn't bothered me a day in my life. For the good God up top gave me a role to play in *this* family's life."

Ralph rolled his eyes but did so good-naturedly, smiling. Charm craned her head all the way back to look up at Betts standing behind her.

"Though, I'll be honest," Betts went on. "I haven't done such a swell job of getting these two to take Jesus seriously. Ralphie's a good father and this is a loving family, but frankly, they only attend Mass on Easter and Christmas— and only then because Ralphie feels obligated. And if the truth is *truly* being told, neither of them prays much, other than when I force them to at this very table. So the point of my pointless yappin' is that I need to be present here more than anyone. The Lord needs devout ears in this room to hear what's about to be told. Someone's got to pray for *real* for these children."

Detective Dave looked a little hurt. "Well, I pray," he said with childlike eyes and that soft gravelly tone. "My wife, my girls, we attend Mass every Sunday."

Ralph chuckled lightly. "Don't mind her, man. Become a bit of an old bat, she has—"

Betts playfully smacked the back of Ralph's head. Charm slapped his arm. He chuckled a bit more.

Betts looked at Detective Dave. "If that's true, I genuinely apologize. But I sure don't see you at my church."

"We attend Saint Luke's Among the Stars, over off Pigeon Pass," Dave said.

"Hmm." Betts considered.

"Um, it's really okay," Charm spoke up. "I want everyone here. I just wanna get it out. Everyone deserves to hear everything."

Dave gave Sherry a single, slow nod, indicating the matter was resolved.

Julia straightened up in her seat, facing Charm. "Billy told me everything he remembers—which is nothing. So please hold nothing back, okay? I promise I won't be angry with you no matter what I hear. Just tell the truth."

"I will."

Officer Sherry released a big, relenting sigh (which everyone ignored) and leaned back against the kitchen counter, her notepad and pen at the ready.

Charm took another deep breath. "Okay. Like I said, Magg and I spent the entire summer apart. We only talked on the phone a few times while I was in the city. I just got back the night before last. I was excited to see her. We had a sleepover planned, and I went over to her house for it."

* * *

Charm had ridden her bike to Maggie-Lynn's house, dropping it on the grass in front of the porch—like she'd done a thousand times before—and knocked on the front door.

She remembered how it almost immediately swung open to reveal her best friend standing there wearing the cheesiest, silliest grin.

I'm so happy you're back, Maggie-Lynn had told her.

And Charm had felt so happy to *be* back, reunited with her partner in crime. Maggie-Lynn, thirteen, always strikingly confident, with big frizzy hair and sharp eyes.

The new girl peeked up from behind Magg's shoulder, smiling wide and waving hello. Twelve-year-old Tildra, who was short, with dark hair and black horn-rimmed glasses. Tildra, who Magg had said over the phone was their long-sought Third, the one who would at last turn their loner duo into a loner trio. After so many years, the hope that they would ever find a Third had taken on an almost mythical quality. It was unexpected news for Charm—and something exciting to look forward to upon arriving home, especially after enduring her little snot-nosed cousins all summer.

A much-wanted newcomer to befriend and hang with and invite to sleepovers and trust their weird secrets to. It had all sounded splendid over the phone.

The trouble was, Charm had no idea then just how influential the new girl had already become.

* * *

"When I got there, that's when I met Tildra," she told the kitchen. "She was already there. We went upstairs in Maggie-Lynn's room and sat on her bed, and Magg, she . . ." Charm couldn't help but chuckle, albeit a bit nervously. "She blew a giant bubble from the gum she was chewing, and she was looking right at me, and she said—with a big grin, she said, 'Do you wanna *prank* Billy Tippard?'"

4

THE FIRST NIGHT

7:39 P.M.

"Okay, here's the thing," Magg said. "There ain't gonna be a sleepover tonight."

The statement caught Charm mid-giggle, and she paused, giving a puzzled smirk of confusion. The three girls had laughed their way excitedly up the stairs and slammed the bedroom door shut behind them, hopping onto Magg's big springy bed and getting comfy, sweeping and kicking the teddy bears and other stuffed animals to the red shag carpet. All three settled cross-legged on the bed, facing each other.

"Er—I mean, there will be later," Magg assured her. "We'll be back before the sun comes up. But we're going on an adventure tonight."

"We have a heavy question for you, Charm," Tildra said. The tall lamp in the corner of the room caught the lenses of her glasses and gave them a shine. Charm couldn't see the new girl's eyes.

Magg blew a giant, see-through red bubble of gum, expanding, expanding, expanding—until it disappeared suddenly with a sharp, loud *POP!*

After which she gave Charm a big grin and said, "Do you

wanna *kill* Billy Tippard?" Her eyes then widened to their brink, and she waited, her expression crazed.

"Yeah, wanna kill him with us?" Tildra followed up. She flashed two rows of almost pointy white teeth under her glared-out glasses, presenting a shiny smile.

It was obvious to Charm that Magg and Tildra had much anticipated this moment, looking forward to her reaction. And Charm knew—could somehow *feel*—that they weren't joking. This was the real deal. She was being directly asked if she wanted to kill someone. And not just any someone, but someone she *knew* for as long as she'd known Magg. Billy Tippard was nice. Sure, he could be a twerp sometimes, like anyone could, but he was harmless. Charm realized she was blinking continuously and stopped. A torrent of chills flared up her spine, and she had to pick her dropped jaw back up from the bedspread. She even felt a little woozy.

But she was also undeniably intrigued and had to know more. "Go on," she said at last.

Magg started smacking her gum again in good cheer. "I ain't pranking you. Couldn't tell you about it over the phone, of course. But it's been all planned out for a good while now. We've just been waiting for you to come home and do it with us."

Charm let out a surprised breath, and a stream of slobber dripped from the corner of her lip down onto her pajama shirt—it was supposed to be a sleepover, after all. The other two chortled as she quickly wiped her mouth.

"We've talked about this for years, Charm, you and I," Magg said. "Let's actually do it. Send someone to the netherworld."

It was true. Charm and Magg had, on occasion, discussed what the thrill of murder would be like. That wasn't so unnatural for them, given their long-shared passion for the macabre. They were straight crime fiends, horror fanatics. They grew up on slasher films and true crime shows and never failed to be enthralled by news stories of grisly murders. But Charm never *seriously* entertained the notion of murder when she and Magg had those discussions (usually during October, leading up to their favorite holiday). She just thought the topic was fun because it was so taboo.

But the human brain was powerful. It could revisit any number of moments from the past in one fraction of a second—usually when one was hit with revelation—and Charm suddenly realized in that fraction of a second that Magg had always been more animated about the prospect of murder than one might think of as mere enthusiasm. Magg would always get sweaty and raise her voice and go wide-eyed as they discussed what their favored murder weapon would be or how exactly they would do the deed. And in that same split-second, Charm figured she must have just always chalked up Magg's spirited behavior to Magg's own exuberant nature.

But maybe there *was* something there, deeper down in Maggie-Lynn, something truly sinister that had always wanted to escape.

Well, heck. Not maybe. Most definitely. Magg and their new friend were planning to kill Billy Tippard—and that was huge. Not to mention twisted and sudden and overwhelming and just plain wrong. So, so wrong. Charm knew that, of course. She breathed deeply, centering herself.

"I'm in," she said.

And that was that.

"You know I'm in," Charm said again, all smiles. "But give me the details first. Tell me how this all came about."

5

THE SECOND NIGHT

Charm sighed at the kitchen table. "And so, well . . ." She swallowed hard, as though struggling to keep down the tears in front of everyone. "They gave me all the details, told me how it all came about. How exactly we were gonna prank him and everything. And I was excited. I wanted to do it. Thought it would be fun."

She hung her head, took in a sharp breath, then continued on with her carefully revised version of the previous night's events. For the moment, Charm was just relieved that her bedroom wasn't getting searched too.

PART II

GEARING UP FOR THE GRAVEYARD

1

—————

THE FIRST NIGHT

"We'll tell you the whole plan in a jiff," Magg assured Charm. "But we gotta catch you up on all the gooey backstory first. Take it away, Tildra."

Tildra sat unmoving on the bed, looking at them with a peaceful expression, both corners of her closed mouth raised up into a relaxed smile—as if she were savoring the last of their initial reveal to Charm and relishing what was already a fond memory.

Suddenly she popped off the bed in a twirl, spinning across the room toward the dresser where she stopped and pulled a black binder from her backpack. She strode back and sat cross-legged again on the bed, hugging the binder protectively in her arms.

"It's an honor to meet you, Charm," she said in a stately, regal manner, chin held high.

"Yeah," Charm agreed with a slow nod, a strange knowing feeling creeping inside of her—a feeling that her life would now be forever changed because of this new person. "Magg said you were just like us on the phone. I had some ideas about what that meant. We've been waiting a long time for a new weirdo to complete our triangle."

Tildra smirked. She suggested they call her Bermuda as a cool nickname, and the three of them shared a feel-good laugh even though they knew the joke was corny.

Then Charm was told the tale of how Magg and Tildra met.

2

___

TWO MONTHS BEFORE THE VIOLENT NIGHTS

11:24 A.M.

There was no sun to be found in the dimly lit public library. Shades drawn, dusty, deserted—a loner's ideal setting for silence and solitude.

With her frizzy hair forced back into a bun and sporting her new cheerleading uniform (her school's mascot, a red fox, emblazoned on the front), Maggie-Lynn walked through the aisles of the library that was like a second home to her. She didn't have any classes to attend. Unlike most of the kids who were in summer school to make up for flunking, Magg's report cards were fine. It was smooth sailing into eighth grade, she was only attending summer school for cheerleading training. After her daily practice, she was free to cross the street and roam the town library until she felt like riding her bike home.

Magg rounded onto her favorite aisle—*TRUE CRIME*, of course—and was surprised to take notice of a stranger browsing through one of the shelves.

She narrowed her eyes, studying Tildra, who wore a plain, baggy T-shirt, blue jeans, and sneakers. Long dark hair concealed her face from the side. She was hunched over, pushing books left and right with both hands, evidently unable to find whatever title she had in mind. Magg could tell the girl wore glasses when one of her hands moved to push them back up.

Magg wondered who this new girl was and why she was looking through this particular aisle. Nobody looked through these shelves with *that* much interest.

Magg stepped forward. "Hi. Which book are you looking for?"

Tildra jolted in place as if struck by lightning, throwing Magg a look like she'd just been caught trying to steal a first edition hardcover. "Uhhhh—"

"I'm familiar with these shelves," Magg said, looking around with pride. "I've read almost everything here." She raised her hands, palms up, presenting the true crime aisle as if it were all her own property. And it might as well have been. Hardly anyone used the library except for her, Charm, and the few other book nerds among the townsfolk.

"You have?" Tildra asked, surprised but curious.

"This stuff's my hobby."

The true crime aisle was filled with a wide-ranging assortment—from historical textbooks about petty crime in ancient Rome to the first accounts of witch trials in Salem— up to more modern tomes that covered murder mysteries and unsolved disappearances.

Tildra raised an eyebrow. "And what hobby is that, exactly?"

Magg hesitated, not knowing how to answer. "Never mind." She gave up. It wasn't worth the risk to expose herself further. "I'm here often if you ever need help, though . . ." And Magg turned, meaning to leave the girl be and come back later.

It was Tildra who took the chance. "I was just seeing if

they had, by any chance, a book about the, umm, Bloody Benders? They were a family of serial killers, lived in Kansas a long time ago—"

"Yeah, the Benders were extraordinary," Magg blurted, turning back around with pure euphoria swelling in her chest.

Tildra looked startled, then intrigued. "You think so?"

Magg composed her thoughts. "Well, they were a close family that killed people together. They would kindly welcome locals who happened upon their inn along the country road, then they'd stab 'em in the face and bash their heads in—as a family. Got away with it for a good while too. But what's *really* fascinating is when they were finally found out—when they knew their jig was up—they disappeared, took off. Vanished, like. Never to be seen again. And it's a true story! If that ain't extraordinary, nothing is."

* * *

Tildra Smith was a private kid; she kept her dark side to herself. She knew very well who the Bloody Benders were, had already read a book about them. She merely desired to find another for supplemental reading. But in that moment, after hearing how this bright-eyed cheerleader who had approached her spoke, Tildra wondered—for the very first time—if she had just met someone like herself.

And what were the chances of that? Meeting someone similar to herself? Someone she could actually open up to? Someone who could maybe be trusted with her secrets— maybe even be useful with her plans?

Tildra smiled. "Well said."

"And there is a library book on the Benders," Magg continued, smiling back. "But my best friend Charm stole it.

It's at her house. That's the best thing about this library: nobody's ever here, books pile up, we take the ones we want, nobody notices. And new books still come in all the time."

"I did notice how packed yet empty it is," Tildra said. "My favorite kind of library."

Magg nodded in a way that said she could relate. "Yeah, my friend Charm and I, we have a big shared collection of books, a bunch in her room and more in mine. It's a pretty creepy collection too. A sort of fun-but-classified hobby of ours. My name's Maggie-Lynn by the way."

Tildra knew a thing or two about keeping things classified. She held out a hand. "I'm Tildra. Just moved to town. I'm actually supposed to be across the street in summer school right now. I failed math. Home ec too. But then I saw the library here and decided to ditch." She gave Magg another smile. "I own a few creepy books myself."

Magg's face lit up, and she shook Tildra's hand up and down several times.

* * *

That very evening in Magg's room, she and Tildra sat across from each other on the floor by her bed. A large bag of potato chips, two cans of soda pop, and a few candy wrappers littered the floor. A stack of a dozen books sat between them: unsolved murder collections, serial killer biographies, even a few tomes Tildra had brought over covering satanic rituals and dark magic.

Tildra had her mysterious black binder held protectively in her arms.

She held up her pinky.

Magg linked her own with it, and the two girls performed the sacred pinky promise.

Tildra handed Magg the binder.

Magg opened it. At first, as she flipped through a few pages of the contents, she kept a stoic face. Then her brows raised. Her eyes widened. Her jaw fell. And she grinned, knowing for sure she'd found a third member to make their trio.

3

———

THE FIRST NIGHT

"Y'all are adorable," Charm said, amused. "Corny, but adorable. I imagined that as the cheesiest—"

"Shut up!" Magg laughed. "We've been waiting for you to get back ever since!"

"I just feel bad now," Charm said with an uneasy smile. "Magg told me to bring that Bender book tonight. I forgot."

Tildra only looked disappointed for a second before turning her frown up into a smile of her own. Charm could tell she was let down but tried not to show it.

"Oh," Tildra mumbled. "It's fine—"

"Darn," Charm said with realization. "You were waiting all summer to read it. I'm sorry. But school starts on Monday! I'll bring it then, I promise."

"No, I promise it really is fine. I'm more happy just to meet you."

"Privilege is mine, fellow weirdo." Charm gave her a sitting bow.

Tildra beamed with great joy, her binder still glued to her chest. "So, Charm," she said, making conversation, "who are your favorite serial killers?"

"Oh, wow." Charm laughed, caught off guard by the question. "I don't know. There's lots of good ones." She tapped her chin in thought. "Personally, I enjoy reading about old, wicked legends. There was this Han dynasty prince from the second century BC, Liu Pengli, who would literally sneak out of the palace at night to hunt random peasants for fun. Ended up being exiled by his father. Pretty neat. And oh, there's Liz Bathory! Transylvanian noblewoman from the 1500s who believed she was a vampire. She bathed in and drank the blood of her six-hundred-plus victims. A lot of her story might be exaggerated, but it's still chilling!"

Maggie-Lynn yawned, nodding in agreement, then she laid back on the bed and allowed the other two girls to get to know each other.

"I think the Benders are the most fascinating, though, for sure," Charm concluded. "Just 'cause we know they were for real."

Tildra regarded Charm, biting her lip. Then she lowered her hands, allowing her black binder to fall with them. With one finger, she flicked open the binder, super slick. "Maggie-Lynn told me a lot about you, Charm. And now I wanna tell you about me. I may come off as nice and sweet—and for the most part, I can be. But make no mistake, I'm also out of my tree." She pulled a piece of white sketch-paper from her binder and handed it to Charm.

It was a penciled sketch of an unknown person lying dead, their head nothing more than a pile of bloody, brainy mush, a pair of broken glasses in the middle of the mess. Next to the body there was also a small sketch of a dripping hammer.

LAZY DOODLE #317 was scribbled in the top-right corner of the page.

"I've always daydreamed about killing people," Tildra said. "My entire life. But I'm not dumb, I don't wanna go to jail—or worse, some mental place. So I found—or made, rather—an outlet for myself. I got real good at fictionally killing people."

"Who is this?" Charm asked, still looking at the sketch.

Tildra shrugged. "Who knows? Some poor bloke from my imagination." She placed a second sheet of white paper on top of the first one in Charm's hands. Another grotesque illustration of violence. This page featured four different sketches of a long-haired, middle-aged woman's face. The first sketch at the top-left of the page was a simple portrait of the woman smiling, oblivious of what was to come. In the second sketch, at the top-right, a dainty hand had a fistful of the woman's long hair, pulling it back hard, stretching the skin thinly over the face, eyes and teeth enlarged for effect.

The third sketch on the bottom-left was the most elaborate, and it reminded Charm of when Betts made her help pull weeds in the yard. The dainty hand had yanked the woman's hair right out of her cranium, root and stem, with terrible force—skin ripped clean off the face as well, hanging from the hair like a hollow, leathery mask, leaving a veil of dripping gray pencil-blood over the remaining skeletal visage.

The fourth sketch on the bottom-right was a simple skull. It was smiling. *LAZY DOODLE #241.*

"Jeezus," Charm said uneasily before letting out a laugh. "You sure can draw! You're real talented."

"I've just had a lot of practice," Tildra said, her tone modest, almost shy. Next in her demonstration, she plucked from within her binder a small but very well-crafted origami of a crying baby, holding it up for Charm to see.

Charm thought it was cute, the body made from beige

construction paper, the diaper made from white, with blue paper teardrops streaming from the closed eyes that Tildra had drawn on with a pen. She'd also drawn a little wailing mouth. Tildra presented the baby to Charm in the middle of her open right palm, just before bringing her left fist down and smashing it, crushing it, ripping it in her hands. She tore the (now deformed) crying head off and tossed the crumpled remnants onto the two drawings Charm still held.

"*For the monster gods*," Tildra whispered, as if in tribute.

Charm slowly craned her head around at Magg. Magg simply nodded back.

"Well," Charm said, turning back to Tildra as she handed the sketches back, "I wouldn't wanna live in your imagination, that's for sure."

Tildra grinned, once again flashing her pearly whites. "Billy Tippard's going to wish he didn't live in our world."

"And we'll oblige him," Magg said. "'Cause he's leaving it!"

"Yikes." Charm cringed. "Y'all *are* corny. But seriously, give me the rundown now. All the particulars. Where the heck did this whole idea even come from?"

Magg smirked. "You know, you might think it'd be oh-so-complicated, committing murder and getting away with it. But it ain't really—so long as you put in the responsible work and effort of thinking it through."

"I agree in a sense," Charm said. "It does need to be done maturely." She cleared her throat. "Erm, so why Billy Tippard?"

Magg's smirk became a full smile, but she didn't answer. Instead, she rose and walked toward her closet, stepping around the strewn stuffed animals they'd earlier swept to the floor. She opened the closet door, hunched over, and pulled out a big purple duffel bag that Charm had never seen before. It had red and black stars all over it that seemed freshly painted.

"Where did you get that?" Charm asked, curious. The design was a marvel. Simple, but effective. Intuitively, she jerked her head back to Tildra. "Did you *make* that?"

"I did," Tildra said. "Or, I mean, I painted it purple, then painted the stars onto it."

"Very cool," Charm complimented.

Magg brought the bag over and dropped it beside the bed. She put her hands on her hips. "You wanna hear the story, Charm?"

"Let's hear the story," Charm said.

Magg turned around and briskly went to her dresser this time. She pulled open the bottom drawer and gathered up a bundle of folded black bedsheets. She stood up. "We didn't choose Billy Tippard. Billy Tippard chose us."

"Ummm . . . how's that?" Charm asked, confused.

"More like he chose Tildra. Took a shine to her in summer school." Magg turned and went to her desk with the big bundle of bedsheets in her arms. She reached down with one hand and pulled open the top drawer. She began shuffling through it, looking for something.

"I would catch him looking at me around school," Tildra said. "One day, during recess, he threw a paper airplane at me. But from the way it hit me in the back, I could tell he threw it soft. We started talking. And honestly, he wasn't too bad at first. I kinda liked him. Billy looks young for his age, which I also kinda liked—I look young for my age—and he really was nice. But later that week, I was watching him at lunch when he thought he was alone, and I saw him pick his nose and eat it. He gobbled it, Charm. Grossed me out so bad I went in circles bending over and dry-heaving— silently so he wouldn't hear me. It also made me mad—and

I'm not one who tends to get upset. He befriended me and then made me gag half to death. So yeah, I'm gonna kill someone for the first time. Him. I mean, I was always eventually going to kill—that's always been the plan—I just thought it'd be when I was older. Billy sped up the process."

Magg was busy muttering to herself, asking where the darn scissors were as she dug through the drawer with her one free hand, the big bundle of sheets in the other.

"That's wild," Charm said, remembering something long lost in the depths of her memory. "In third grade, I saw him wipe one under his desk one time. I never told anyone."

"*Jesus Christ*," Magg said with disgust. She spat her gum into the desk drawer and slammed it shut, her red scissors hanging off one finger.

Tildra also wore a look of revulsion, staring right through Charm and into nothingness, unblinking, her nostrils flaring in and out. Billy must've really scarred her.

"I've never liked him," Magg said. "Ever since he sneezed on me that one time, years back. He deserves to die." With a flick of her wrists, she unfurled her big bundle of sheets across the floor. "So anyhow, after the booger incident, we thought, 'Well hell, if we can come up with the right plan, maybe we could kill him.'"

"So what's the right plan?" Charm asked.

"See," Magg continued, "the thing is, Tildra's been leading Billy on."

"I haven't let him kiss me or anything," Tildra quickly added. "But he wants to."

"Right," Magg concurred. "And we're gonna use that. Billy thinks tonight's his night. And it is—just not in the way he believes. He's sneaking out to meet Tildra. Tildra told him she wants to talk to him about something important, and I told him that means she wants to kiss him. Long story short, when he meets up with her, we're gonna knock him out, kidnap and kill him."

Charm snorted. "I think I'll need to hear more details than just that."

"Sure, sure. Of course." Magg sat down cross-legged on the carpet and began carefully cutting away at one of the black sheets with her red scissors. "We got a few hours yet. Ask away."

Charm did wonder what the heck Magg was doing cutting up her own bedsheets, but amidst the more pressing matter of planning a so-called murder, she didn't care enough to ask. There were far more important things to query. "Well, where's he meeting Tildra? And has he *told* anyone he's meeting Tildra? How are we gonna kill him? With *what* are we gonna kill him? And most importantly: How are y'all planning on making positive we don't get caught?"

"He's meeting her at the overgrown graveyard," Magg said.

"The old Civil War cemetery," Tildra added for clarity.

"Oh, I know it." Charm gave Magg a deadly stare.

Magg chuckled, cutting away at the black sheet.

Tildra looked back and forth at the two of them, curious. "What?"

Magg didn't even look up from her cutting as she answered. "I scared the heck out of Charm there one time. We were eleven. We snuck out to the graveyard in the middle of the night 'cause I dared her. It was after we both read about the infamous graveyard murders of Chickasaw Ridge."

"What happened!?" Tildra was overwhelmed with excitement, her face lit up.

"She left me alone, then waited for me to walk by and

jumped out of a tree, right over my head, screaming like a demon," Charm said.

Magg laughed. "I jumped off a branch and tackled her to the ground. Her eyes were shut, and she was shouting, 'Ahhhh! Betts! Daddy! Betts! Ahhhhhhh!'"

"Ohhhh." Tildra marveled at that, turning back to Charm. "She got you good."

"That she did, yeah," Charm admitted.

"I wanna meet Betts. Maggie-Lynn's told me a little bit about her. She sounds interesting."

"That she is, yeah. She's a Bible-thumper, but she ain't all strict about it. She lets me do what I want."

"Does she know about your and Maggie-Lynn's secret book collection?"

"No," Charm said softly, surprised. "She doesn't go in my room. She always says, 'Our privacy is ours and ours alone.'"

"Yeah, she sounds cool. What's your old man like?"

"Hard worker on the job, lazy bum at home. Why?"

Tildra shook her head with a shrug and a smile. "Magg said as much when I asked her all about you. Just wanting to get to know you for myself."

Magg finished her cutting of the first sheet. She gathered it up and tossed it in a corner. "Billy's meeting Tildra at midnight on top of the big hill in the graveyard," she said. "We're gonna hit him on the head with a branch, carry him to the old restroom—and then that's where the fun begins." She picked up one end of a second black sheet, making sure it was spread evenly across the floor, and again went cutting away. The constant snip, snip, *sniiiip* sounds of the scissors added a soothing white noise to the room.

Charm tried to appear relaxed, unaware of how tense she actually was, sitting hunched and cross-legged all this time. She still didn't know *how* Magg and Tildra were planning to kill Billy, but for the moment she found herself more concerned with how they were planning to cover their tracks. "Okay, so we kill him," she said. "I'm good with that. Good family fun. But then what? After, I mean. How do we make sure—"

"It doesn't really matter who Billy tells about meeting up with Tildra," Magg said. "Tildra doesn't *need* to keep it a secret. If the powers that be ask, she'll just tell 'em Billy never showed up. That's what her story's gonna be, if she needs to tell it. Huh, Tildra?"

Tildra leapt off the bed again, hopping over the stuffed animals lying about as she went and picked up her backpack off the dresser. "I did ask Billy not to tell anyone about tonight—and I trust him. But don't worry, Charm. After we kidnap him, we can make him tell us if he blabbed or not. And believe me, we'll know if he's lying." She winked at Charm, then brought her backpack across the room and sat on the floor beside the purple duffel bag with red and black stars all over it.

Magg once again took over the proceedings. "Basically, we're gonna do the deed in the old bathroom and leave his body there. But what we ain't gonna leave there is any evidence of us." With her scissors hand she gestured to the duffel bag beside Tildra. "We got gloves and everything. Special clothes just for the occasion. I got us all shoes too. We're gonna burn the clothes after. We won't leave a trace of us. No trace."

Tildra zipped open the duffel bag and pulled right from the top a clear plastic bag with a dark sweater, jeans, and socks stuffed in it, all folded up tight. Then she reached in and pulled out a fresh pair of shoes, still linked with the plastic strip. Black sneakers. She tossed the bag and shoes to Charm.

"Here's your getup," Tildra told her. "Just like us." Tildra wore a dark blue sweater and black jeans, Magg a black sweater and blue jeans. Charm hadn't registered until then just how closely they were dressed.

"Wow," Charm said, surprised and slightly impressed. "Okay. Wow."

Charm shifted and hung her legs off the side of the bed, changing from the cross-legged position she had been sitting in this entire time—and it suddenly felt like a thousand fuzzy needlepoints were stinging her legs all over.

"Ahhh," she mumbled. "My legs fell asleep."

Tildra spoke softly from the floor. "Basically, Billy's going missing tomorrow. And we're all gonna be horrified. Everyone will be talking about it at school on Monday. After a day or two at most, they'll start a search. After another day or two, they'll find his body in the rusty restroom at the old, overgrown graveyard. And we'll all be devastated." She pretended to tear up with fake sniffles. "Cue the waterworks. I had a crush on him, remember . . ."

They all laughed, then Magg shot Charm a devilish look. "You and I might even go to his funeral. We've known him for so long."

"Half the school will probably go," Tildra said. "I plan to be there." She then produced from her backpack a brand-new three-piece stainless steel knife set, still wrapped in the see-through plastic packaging. There was a big, 12-inch hunting knife, a 9-inch serrated knife, and a small, 2-inch pocketknife.

Charm gasped with the realization that these were to be the murder weapons.

While Tildra was putting the knife set into the duffel bag, Charm also glimpsed some of the bag's additional contents: a flashlight, several pairs of black leather gloves, a roll of purple duct tape, two black throw pillows, and at least three small lanterns.

Charm looked at Magg. "Okay, I'm sorry if this was already explained, but what if Billy *did* tell someone he's meeting Tildra? Wouldn't admitting to being at the graveyard make her the first suspect?"

Magg answered. "If Billy told anyone, then Tildra tells the tale."

Charm frowned. "Which is what again?"

"I already told you. Billy never showed up. Right, Tildra?"

Tildra got into character as if she were speaking to a room full of grown-ups, her face sad and serious. "Right. I waited for a long time. Up on the big hill where we agreed to meet." She sniffled. "We were gonna hang out, explore, have fun. And I was gonna kiss him."

Charm chuckled.

"Wiser to just admit she was at the graveyard," Magg said. "In the long run, appearing to be forthcoming and honest about it will give her more credibility, even with how it might look. Again, this would only be if Billy did blab."

Tildra pulled a Walkman from her backpack and ejected a cassette tape. She spun the tape up in the air for fun and caught it. Then, in two steps—a skip and a hop—she stood before Magg's fancy new boombox on her bedside table. Tildra's cassette had a white label on it, and on that label, written in black marker, Charm eyed the words: *MAGICAL MURDER MIX.*

Tildra popped the cassette into the tape deck of the boombox and punched play.

The classical-sounding music was unfamiliar to Charm. But while cutting away at the sheet, Magg began swaying her head as if listening to a childhood favorite, even though

Charm knew for sure Magg had never heard it before meeting Tildra either.

It was a wicked, sinister melody, and beautiful. Ominous but with a sensitive grace to it. The faint lyrics were an indecipherable chanting, high but soft—like fiendish fairies from a dark forest perhaps. Or just something from a lost, ancient realm. Something, Charm thought, that might be performed ceremoniously before (or after) a fight to the death, or during a full solar eclipse while a sacrifice was made to the gods.

Charm began swaying her own head to it.

Magg finished her careful cutting of the second black sheet. She gathered it up and tossed it over on top of the first. She picked up the corner of the third and final sheet and again went snipping away.

Tildra sat back down on the floor between her backpack and the purple duffel bag. She looked up at Charm. "I'm confident Billy didn't tell anyone. I've gotten to know him. He has no reason to go against what I want. He wants me to like him."

Charm bobbed her head here and there, thinking about it. "Yeah, okay. I see that."

And she did see it. She knew Billy too. He was easy enough to be around. He could be a real *boy* sometimes, burping and farting, but he was good-natured, never cruel, and Charm believed he was trustworthy enough to keep a secret. Not that it mattered so much—it was Tildra taking all the real risk, not Charm or Magg.

"What if we're spotted around town tonight?" Charm asked. "While riding our bikes."

"We always ride our bikes," Magg said, as if the question was dumb. "But we won't be spotted with Billy, and that's what counts. Also, anyone that might see us would be just as much of a suspect—because what were *they* doing out so late, you know? No one's gonna say anything."

Tildra suddenly raised her right hand straight up above her head like a kid in class and held it there for a moment, wiggling and curling her fingers before bringing the hand back down and burying it deep into her backpack, like a cobra diving into a dark ground-tunnel. The stylistic movement enraptured Charm because she instinctively knew that whatever Tildra was reaching for must be something worth the dramatics. And it was.

Tildra pulled out three masks one by one, slowly and gently setting them each down on the carpet, face-up.

The masks were made of paper mâché, and all three were identical. Shaped into human skulls, they were purple, with large red teardrops streaming from the eyeholes. They also had plain leather stretch-straps along the back.

Charm always thought that human skulls had a natural smile going on about them, and she guessed Tildra felt the same way because she'd carved an extra bit of grin into the cheeks for stylization. Charm knew without even having to ask that Tildra had made these masks, each one looking like it was beaming right back at you with its dead face, crying happy red tears. Overall, they were pretty darn creepy. Tildra had done a good job.

"What are *those* for?" Charm asked.

"We're gonna wear them when we torture Billy," Tildra said.

"We're really gonna *torture* Billy?"

"Sure are," Tildra said. "What's the point of killing someone for fun if you're gonna make it quick?"

Charm blinked, having no genuine reply to that. "Damn," she said. "Touché. But . . . why the masks? And what's with the sheets, Magg? What are you cutting them up for?"

"Well . . ." Tildra started.

Magg looked up from her sheet-cutting, wide-eyed. It was apparent that she knew what Tildra was about to say and was eager to witness it being told to Charm.

"We're wearing this stuff," Tildra said. "These masks, and those black sheets made into robes, for the ritual killing taking place tonight. We're gonna start a new generation of unsolved murders. Real stuff of legend brought back to life. Like the Bloody Benders, but better—we're not just unknown serial killers. We're gonna do secret society stuff. We'll be organized. We'll craft nightmares and haunt whoever we want. And what we carry out is gonna stand the test of time forever." Tildra's eyes blazed behind her glasses. "We're creating the occult in this town. I've spent years dreaming up and writing down a whole mythology—ruled by cosmic monster gods. And what we do is by their will. This, Charm, is my life's work."

Charm stared at her. Then she turned her head to Magg with a half-hearted, almost disbelieving giggle, not knowing how to react.

Magg spoke softly. "I told you on the phone that she was just like us. Hell, she's more us than *us*."

Charm looked back at Tildra and saw she had her hand held out for Charm to shake. Charm took it instantly. They'd finally found their Third, Charm thought. Much more of a Third than she ever thought possible, though.

"Now, get dressed," Magg said to Charm. "We still got time, but let's not waste it. And we gotta get your hair in a bun. All three of us, matter o' fact."

4

9:37 P.M.

From the boombox on the bedside table, Tildra's "Magical Murder Mix" now played the "Lacrimosa" sequence of Mozart's *Requiem in D minor*. Haunting, majestic, and dark, Maggie-Lynn recognized the music—as many would—but couldn't personally place its identity. Regardless, she thought it was sublime and allowed herself to bask in the fitting ambience.

Along one wall of her room in the center of two enormous piles of clothes (one clean, one filthy) stood a tall standing mirror. Magg, her hair in a tight bun, examined herself before it. She was wearing one of the black sheets. It covered her entire body, save her head. The hemline of the sheet around her feet was cut upward into flaps to her knees.

She forgot to cut armholes.

"At least it fits, I guess," she mumbled to herself. She flapped her arms underneath the sheet.

In the reflection of her mirror she spied Charm and Tildra sitting on the floor cross-legged, talking together. She also eyed in the reflection a framed picture on the far wall of herself and Charm hugging when they were much younger.

Magg smiled. She was happy, excited, and ready for a monumental night.

* * *

With Tildra's long dark hair in a big bun and Charm's short sandy hair in a little bun, the two now wore their own black sheet-robes (no armholes) as they sat together, talking.

Tildra had put in contact lenses just before donning the makeshift robe, placing her horn-rimmed specs in her back-pack for the night. "So the ritual is real simple," she said, her bare eyes gleaming. "First time in the field, best we keep it simple. We're basically just gonna say some scary stuff to him before going wild with the knives. We'll give you the details as it goes, and you can just follow along."

"What kind of scary stuff?"

"It's all from the mythology I've written. Stuff to make him believe in monsters."

Charm giggled. "Wow. This is like a front-row seat to the greatest show on Earth."

Tildra giggled back. Then she told Charm the name of their secret society.

Charm's eyebrows shot up, impressed. "I like it. Tildra, how do you come up with all this stuff?"

Tildra thought about it a moment, looking away. "I do research, pull stuff from books. But a lot of it is drawn from dreams I have. Daydreams, oftentimes. Just staring off into space. But also nightdreams too." She shrugged. "Stuff shows up, I put it to paper."

A minute later, Magg turned away from her mirror and

looked down upon her two best friends. "After the cops find Billy's body at the graveyard, Tildra will come forward *if* she has to, shocked and inconsolable about how she was there that night too to meet up with him, but he never showed up. She'll feel so guilty about what happened—that he went missing coming to meet her. But how could she have known that at the time? She thought he bailed on her! And then—get this, Charm, this is the best part—Tildra will remember how she saw a cloaked figure in the trees that night. But when she took a second look, there was nothing there, so she thought she was just seeing things."

"And the legend will be born of the cloaked man at the graveyard," Tildra added. "He killed Billy but didn't kill me. I don't know why. Maybe because I was on my bike when I glimpsed him, and he didn't wanna have to chase me. So he hid." She waved away her own reasoning. "In any case, I was lucky. It could just as easily have been me."

"That's right," Magg said.

Charm considered. "I'm buying it, I'm buying it. Might be a few folks in town who'll suspect you, Tildra—at least for a little while. But most in their right minds won't."

The girls all traded approving nods as Magg joined them on the floor, sitting cross-legged.

"Tildra likely won't even have to come forward," Magg said casually. "I bet Billy kept his mouth shut. But we'll just play out the next few days and see what happens—"

"We've known Billy since first grade," Charm blurted out matter-of-factly.

Magg burst out a laugh. "I know!"

Tildra was suddenly giddy, rocking back and forth and side to side with a wide-eyed grin, giggling. The other two stared at her.

"I get silly when I'm excited," Tildra said, flapping her arms under her sheet. And just as suddenly, she stopped rocking and went still. She gave Magg an accusatory look. "You spent all this time with them scissors and didn't cut any armholes? Really?"

5

MIDNIGHT

The Milky Way was like a deep gash in the night sky. A cosmic slash across the expanse. For some reason, it seemed to emit a strange reddish hue that night, as if bleeding in space. Elsewhere scattered about were thousands of visible stars—twinkling, shimmering, sparkling, like diamond bits drifting through a purple-black sea. At the bottom of the sky, in the far-off distance, an itsy-bitsy bolt of crooked lightning struck the earth somewhere silently. From the trees, the soft hooting of a great horned owl rang out through the clear air. The night was dark, but there was more than enough starlight to see.

Billy Tippard walked through the graveyard.

The name of the cemetery—if there ever was one—went unknown among Civil War historians, as any original sign or documentation for the grounds had long since been lost. Regardless, for many years, every spring, the town would gather in a large clearing on the land and perform poor reenactments of old Rebel-versus-Yankee skirmishes. This was back when Betts was around Julia Tippard's age. But that tradition faded over time, and now decades of abandonment had led to nature's chaos at the cemetery. Overgrown trees, shrubs, and bushes ran rampant, with poison ivy and dandelions everywhere, and countless gravestones lost under the mud. Only the taller memorials and granite obelisks had survived the test of time.

But there was a stone path that endured. Wide and well-made, it led right up to the top of a big hill in the center of the cemetery grounds. This was where Billy now marched, about halfway up the trek. The air was calm and still, holding its breath.

Out to Billy's left there was a vast, wild pumpkin patch, grown out of control like everything else. The sight of it astounded him. Halloween season was right around the corner, and some of those pumpkins were *huge*. Many were rotting he could tell, slowly turning the color of mold. But they were all bigger than any jack-o'-lantern he'd ever seen on someone's doorstep, that was for sure.

And to his right, should Billy have chosen to look in that direction at that particular moment along the path, he would have seen Charm's blank, stone-cold face watching him through an open hole in the dense foliage she was hiding behind, a mere few feet away.

He didn't look, though.

Billy walked with his hands in his pockets. He wore a clean pair of denim jeans and a plain hoodie, pulled up over his always-messy hair. He was thirteen, but he knew he looked ten. Puberty hadn't been smooth sailing for him; his voice was still light and frilly while everyone else's in school had gotten deep, and he was shorter than even most of the girls.

But none of that bothered him anymore after Tildra said she liked those things about him. That was back on the day they met during recess, when she had thrown a paper airplane at him, and they had started talking.

"Please, God," he wished under his breath as he marched along. "Let me get some tongue tonight. Please, please, God. Bless me . . . with Tildra's tongue."

He followed the path right up to the top of the hill where a small shadowy figure sat atop the tallest gravestone in the cemetery, waiting for him. An ancient yew tree with long sprawling branches loomed large behind that gravestone, casting the sitting figure in night-shade.

* * *

The grave plot was that of some general or other, its thick rectangular pillar of a memorial rising several meters into the air, the words *FOR THE UNION* engraved into the stone.

Tildra sat atop it cross-legged, hidden in shadow. She wasn't wearing the black sheet; she was back in just her sweater and jeans for the time being, hair still in a tight bun.

Billy was eight or nine steps from the tombstone pillar, looking up at her.

He smiled, curious. "Tildra?"

Tildra sat unmoving, keeping her face hidden. "Hi, Billy."

Billy beamed with delight. "Hi! You look nice, sitting up there like that. I actually can't see your face, but I'm sure it's still cute."

"Did you tell anyone at all that you'd be coming here tonight?"

"What? No. I didn't. You said not to."

"Okay. I believe you. Listen, I'm going to be candid with you, William. I'd like to start my own collection of pet hamsters."

That caught Billy off guard, his head cocked. "Uhh . . . What? Okay, umm . . . sure, I like hamsters. Why hamsters, though?"

* * *

Maggie-Lynn hid hunched behind the tombstone pillar, out of Billy's sight. She was also back in just her sweater and jeans with her hair in a bun. She peeked around the tombstone.

Tildra answered Billy. "I'm gonna start with a boy hamster. I'll name him Bill. And then after the next sacrifice, I'll get another hamster. A boy if it's a boy and a girl if it's a girl, and name it whoever that person's name is, and so on. Since I plan on being responsible, there'll probably be a lot of time in between new hamsters, so the collection likely won't ever get too big to handle." The last part sounded more to herself. "Plenty of time in between hamsters to reflect on how they behave. Take notes, learn. Perfect the craft."

Billy smiled. "Well . . . I don't really know what the heck you're talking about, but I know I ain't Bill or William. Bill is short for William, and William is my deadbeat dad. I'm just Billy."

Tildra did not respond.

Billy took a step forward, pulling down the hood of his sweater and looking a little concerned now. "Tildra, can I see your face?"

Magg stepped out from behind the grave pillar, clicking on her flashlight. She shined the light right into Billy's eyes. "I can see *your* face, Billy Tippard," she said. "You know what it looks like?"

Billy put a hand in front of his eyes, shielding himself

from the shine. "Huh!?" he uttered. "Maggie-Lynn? That you?"

"It looks like this." And Magg performed, contorting her facial features and giving an unseeing Billy a terrible impression of him in a high, uneven voice, her free arm flailing about wildly. "*I'm Billy! I don't know what's goin' on!*"

"What's goin' on?" Billy asked.

Charm Wilson, hair in a tight bun and dressed in the sweater, jeans, and shoes that Maggie-Lynn had provided her, suddenly stood behind Billy with nothing less than a giant pumpkin hoisted above her head with two gloved hands.

Billy hadn't noticed her, but *that's* what was going on.

Charm brought the pumpkin down and smashed it onto Billy's unsuspecting head. It broke open over his cranium and the boy crumbled, falling to the ground unconscious, covered in pumpkin guts. Magg had her light on him the whole time.

Tildra unfurled herself from the cross-legged position and leaned off the tombstone pillar, gracefully dropping nine or ten feet down to the ground and landing without a sound. She and Magg walked over to Charm, and the three of them stood in a triangle around Billy. Big chunks and little pieces of pumpkin remnants laid haphazardly all about him, half a dozen seeds stuck to his close-eyed, knocked-out face. Magg kept the light shining on him.

"A pumpkin?" Tildra asked.

"Yeah," Charm said, a little enthusiastic. "I saw the pumpkins and I just, you know—I knew it would be best. Hit him with a pumpkin."

"But he's got the guts all on him now," Magg pointed out. "Why didn't you just use a branch, like we said?"

"I couldn't really find a good one."

Magg looked around. "You couldn't find a *branch*?"

"I just figured a pumpkin would do the job better," Charm insisted. "I bet I could've killed him with a big enough branch. A not-so-big branch might not have knocked him out. Then I would've had to hit him over and over again and, I don't know, man, I saw all the pumpkins and it just felt right."

"It sure worked right," Tildra said, nudging his waist with her foot.

Magg considered. "Can't argue with that, I guess. But I'm carrying him by his legs." She pointed at Charm. "*You* deal with the guts."

* * *

At the bottom of the hill there stood a derelict public restroom built from red brick generations earlier. And on that first violent night, while the stars were shining bright as could be—not a cloud in sight—Charm and Magg carried Billy's unconscious body down the stone path toward that brick restroom, while Tildra skipped and hopped alongside them.

"You like how your hamster spiel went?" Magg asked with a huff, carrying Billy by the legs. "I know you were worried about it. I thought it went great."

"In hindsight, it was kinda tacky," Tildra admitted, skipping along. "I knew it might be—first time in the field and everything. I'll think o' something better next time."

A dozen yards or so behind them, just off the stone path, a red fox darted like lightning from one large bush to another, a young cottontail rabbit hanging limp from its mouth.

6

THE SECOND NIGHT

"Tildra made me and Magg hide outside while she led Billy into the restroom," Charm told the kitchen. She was taking her time, dragging the story out as slowly as she could, making eye contact with everyone, giving detail where she was able, lying when she needed to, all while skipping over any incriminating truths. "Tildra told me the prank was that she was gonna try to get him to take his clothes off 'til he was naked or close to it, then she'd run out of there with his clothes and strand him naked. Then he'd finally get the hint that Tildra didn't like him back."

Charm had thought up the cover story on her bike ride back home the night before, after everything had happened. It was simple, believable—and though it was a rather mean cover (it had to be) and might embarrass Billy, it couldn't possibly be as humiliating for him as the booger-eating truth of why Tildra had wanted to kill him in the first place. *That* embarrassing truth she would do him a favor and keep secret—so long as he held up his end.

She shut her eyes hard, pushing tears back down with might and swallowing another huge breath of shame, lost in her performance. "And again, I didn't care. I just thought it'd be funny. But then it turned out it wasn't a prank at all. Magg and Tildra just made that part up." She hung her head again. "And that's about when they sprung the truth on me. What they'd actually been planning all summer while I was in the city."

7

THE FIRST NIGHT

When Billy Tippard opened his eyes, he was on the floor, sitting up with his back against the wall. Remarkably, his head didn't hurt much. It was almost numb. A dull throb.

Several small lanterns were placed spaced out around an old, out-of-order restroom, the red-yellow lights joining to create one vast, red-gold glow, illuminating the dirty brick walls. Four toilet stalls lined one side (two doors missing, the other two barely on their hinges), the opposite side lined with rusted-bronze sinks and cracked, mud-caked mirrors. Shards of brown glass rested in the sinks and on the ground below. Cobwebs covered every corner.

The scent in his nose was fitting but unexpected at first. It didn't smell like a bathroom. It actually smelled sort of . . . not bad. An earthy, wild rust.

There was a single bare window higher up on one wall, the shimmering stars still visible outside, shining bright.

And right in front of Billy sat a cloaked figure. They held a pencil in one shadowy hand, drawing something in a binder. This figure was garbed in a long, billowing black robe, and bore the head of a human skull—a purple skull, with bloody tears streaming from its eyes.

And in those eyes, Billy Tippard saw the face of death.

He realized they were Tildra's eyes.

* * *

Tildra and Billy were in the restroom alone. After Magg and Charm had secured the boy to the floor, Tildra asked them to wait outside.

Charm Wilson did not know this part of the tale.

While waiting for Billy to wake, Tildra touched up a sketch in her binder. When Billy finally stirred, she looked up. He glanced around for a moment, then focused his sight on her. They shared a momentary stare.

Billy lunged forward, his brow furrowed in distress, only to just realize his hands were bound above his head, taped to a thick, sturdy pipe that ran along the brick wall. Magg and Charm had also bent and forced his legs into a cross-legged position and wrapped nearly the full roll of purple duct tape around his lower half, below the waist. He still had some dried-up pumpkin guts on his hoodie and a seed stuck to the center of his right cheek.

He began clamoring unintelligible pleas through the duct tape over his mouth, eyes welling up with water.

Tildra dropped her masked gaze back to her binder, setting the pencil down. She clicked open the binder loops and fumbled around with her papers, ignoring Billy's whimpers. After getting situated, she looked back up at him.

She held up a drawing in front of his face. It was one of her most recent illustrations of violence—*LAZY DOODLE #398*. Billy squinted at it, looking confused, as if unable to recognize or even understand what was being shown to him.

"You see that?" Tildra said, referring to the drawing. "It's a glimpse of the future. It really is. But this future is a secret for now—so you'll keep it low-key, won't you?" She used her free hand to put a gloved finger in front of her skull mouth, gesturing in jest for Billy to keep what he just saw to himself.

Tildra placed the drawing back down in her binder before picking up a separate piece of paper. "Now, you don't gotta keep this next one secret. This next one concerns *you.*" She showed the paper to Billy.

He looked at the second drawing, staring at it. His eyes widened in horror. He bellowed as loud as he could through the duct tape—for all the good it did him, coming out as nothing more than a low, muffled groan.

It was a sketch of Billy looking just the way he was at that moment: hands bound above his head, duct tape across his mouth and wrapped around his legs. But that wasn't all. In the illustration, an eyeball hung from his left socket and rested against his cheek, and his face was morbidly cut up. His ears were sliced off, resting at other corners of the page. Three different-sized knives were also sketched around him in a triangle. *LAZY DOODLE #399.*

Tildra pushed her mask up on top of her head, the mask's strap hooked under her bun, keeping it in place. She didn't worry about removing her mask in front of Billy. Tildra didn't wear the regalia to stay disguised; she wore it for her own pleasure, to scare her victim. She had accomplished that. Sweating profusely, her adrenaline was pumped. She grinned at Billy, high on life, experiencing what very few people ever do: the joy of their true calling.

Billy squirmed and writhed and hummed screams through the duct tape as fiercely as he could, all to no avail. With all his strength mustered, he could barely even budge.

In one corner of the musty restroom lay the purple duffel bag with red and black stars painted onto it, unzipped, with the knife set in its unopened plastic packaging sitting just visible at the top.

AN UNSCHEDULED
INTERMISSION

1

―――――

THE SECOND NIGHT

"So after a bit," Charm said, "Tildra came back out and said she was ready for us to come inside and see."

"Okay, yeah," Julia Tippard said anxiously. She leaned forward, bracing herself against the table and taking a breath. "I need a minute. A break. I can tell we're getting close to my son's assault. It's a bit overwhelming."

Officer Sherry was a tad annoyed but pretended not to be by giving a big cheesy smile of support. She quickly realized how absurd such an expression would look and let it evaporate before anyone saw.

To Sherry, the child was telling it well, and full of detail. How she had met Tildra the night before in Maggie-Lynn's room and was easily swayed into joining their prank on Billy. She relayed the story of how Maggie-Lynn and Tildra had met, bonding over their shared interest in macabre reading material. She explained how Billy was lured to the graveyard under the pretense of meeting up with Tildra for a kiss. Tildra had led him into the bathroom and had Maggie-Lynn and Charm wait outside. And now they were close to the meat of Charm's story. A break, even for just a moment, was unnecessary—and another reason the interview should have been private.

"Absolutely, yes, of course," Detective Dave said, accommodating. "It's understandable. We can take an intermission. A quick intermission, no problem."

Sherry was full-on annoyed now but hid it well this time, merely nodding in faux agreement—and without displaying another goofy smile.

Betts opened a cupboard. This time, instead of the glass etched with white rabbits she had grabbed for Julia, she selected a glass with a red fox hand-painted onto it. She turned and filled it up at the sink.

"Okay, I'm all right," Julia said. "I just need a moment to collect myself—just need a cigarette is all."

Ralph nodded at that. "Shit, me too."

As Julia and Ralph stood up from the table and left, Betts placed the glass of water in front of Charm.

"Moisten your esophagus," Betts told her. "It seems you still have some story to tell."

Charm obeyed and took a drink.

"So, Charm," Sherry said, casual as could be. "How'd you like the city? Visiting your cousins?"

Betts gave Sherry a sour look. A how-dare-you-have-her-speak-when-I-want-her-to-soothe-her-throat type of look. Sherry didn't notice.

"I go every summer," Charm answered. "They're all little —oldest is ten. So I have to watch 'em a lotta the time. Doesn't really feel like a vacation most days. But they're family, it's fine. Good bookstore down the road too. Has a lot of neat stuff."

With one long fingernail, Betts tapped the glass of water Charm was holding, indicating to her to finish it. Charm obeyed, downing the glass.

Betts went to the fridge and flicked open the cupboard above it. Officer Sherry spotted a bottle of wine and some liquor stashed away. Yet it was only a silver cigarette case Betts grabbed.

Detective Dave was busy jotting away in his portfolio, brows furrowed.

"What are you writing?" Charm almost whispered.

Dave glanced at her, then looked back down and kept his pen moving. "As you tell us what happened, I have to take notes, naturally. But since I gotta take 'em quick, I usually just jot the gist. When I have time, I go back and fill in the blanks."

Charm looked up at Officer Sherry.

Sherry smiled back, holding up her notepad and pen. "Oh, I haven't written anything down yet. I just like to be ready."

Detective Dave closed the portfolio. He pulled a soft pack of cigarettes from his inside jacket pocket just as Betts produced a long slim cigarette from her silver case.

"Guess it's smokes all around," Dave said as he stood.

Betts struck a match, lighting her long cigarette right there next to the fridge—a great red fridge, adorned with a fine collection of high-end magnets Betts had built up over the years. Some were animals. A porcelain fox magnet, a sparkling rabbit, an emerald owl. A picture magnet with an ornate purple frame that had held a photo of Charm and Maggie-Lynn now held a photo of only Charm, switched out just that morning. There were many more magnets. A dozen or so were a set of exquisite see-through crystal stars, different sizes and shades—red, black, other colors.

Dave seemed to admire the collection for a moment, then gave Betts a friendly look. "So, you're allowed to smoke in the house, eh?"

Betts took a long, deep drag, holding the smoke in her lungs until it evaporated. When she replied, there was nothing to exhale, and all she said was, "Rank has its privileges."

Detective Dave nodded. "I can relate to that." He looked at Sherry. "Join me outside."

* * *

Ralph and Julia stood just in the front porch's doorway, which was only one step off from the kitchen. He offered her a smoke from his pack, which she accepted, then pulled out another for himself. Julia struck a match, lit hers, lit his. They exhaled their smoke clouds into the dry evening air. They didn't speak much at first, both feeling a little uncomfortable, having met many times over the years at school functions and birthday parties but never really getting to know each other.

A modest wooden toolshed Ralph had built years earlier sat next to the main house in the Wilson family's front yard. Beyond that yard, the gravel road of their street stretched out of sight in either direction, with all the other little houses making up their neighborhood sitting diagonally along each side, tall grass and shrubs and trees in between. The air was calm, the sky cloudless. It was just past sunset, but the stars were already shining bright, the Milky Way fantastically visible on another clear, moonless night.

Officer Sherry approached Ralph and Julia while they stood in the doorway, awkwardly asking if she and Dave could be pardoned to go out to the yard. Behind Sherry, Dave shook his head at Ralph with an embarrassed shrug. Ralph and Julia moved aside.

"Billy's gonna come over in a bit and say thank you to

Charm," Julia said to Ralph as the two cops walked off. "He was on the phone with his daddy when I left the house. Said he was gonna make a grilled cheese after and ride his bike over later." She let out a surprised laugh like she couldn't believe it. "Brat's lucky he almost died last night, otherwise he'd be grounded for life for sneaking out."

Ralph smiled and exhaled smoke porch-side. "What line o' work's your husband in again?"

"He ain't my husband. He's Billy's daddy."

"Oh?"

"I have a boyfriend."

"Oh."

"Billy stays with his daddy on the weekends. Next town over."

"I guess not this weekend though, right?"

Julia breathed out a cloud and gave Ralph a stare.

"Shit, I'm sorry, I . . ." With his cigarette hand, he motioned over to Officer Sherry, who was down the yard with Detective Dave. "You saw earlier. I ain't good with the way I come across to people."

She sighed. "It's fine. His daddy is a scumbag. Flakes all the time."

* * *

Detective Dave took a fast puff. "Jesus, Sherry. You gotta watch the way you come across to people."

They stood at the end of the yard by the black and blue wagons they rode in on.

"This is my first case, Dave," Officer Sherry said. "And I'm grateful for you showing me the ropes. But it's still my case."

"Might be your first case, but I'm still in charge." He took another quick drag. "Look, you gotta put yourself in our citizens' shoes, understand? You gotta say to them what you know they'll be okay with hearing. That's how good police work works."

Sherry tilted her head, creased her eyebrows, and gave his statement a moment of genuine consideration. Then, "Yeah, I'm not sure I agree with that."

He ignored her. "We'll get the rest of Charm's statement, exonerate her, then we head back to the crime scene, start taking pictures. Gonna be a long night."

"How come you said all six of us were there earlier? At the crime scene? Half of us have the day off today, even the chief."

"Sherry, what did I just teach you?"

"Nothing. I didn't agree."

Dave huffed with an exasperated smile, shaking his head.

Sherry changed the subject. "What exactly does that boy remember? Billy?"

Dave took another lightning-fast puff. "Nothing. Getting hit on the head with a pumpkin."

"A *pumpkin*?"

"Once I think we've been thorough, we'll get it cleaned up." He was talking more to himself now. "And then life goes on, I guess. Tragedy."

"Wait, why didn't I interview Billy with you?"

"It's more or less open and shut, Sherry. I put you on last minute for some quick experience." Detective Dave took in a long, deep drag for once, exhaling an enormous cloud, coughing. "Now, the other two girls, imagine interviewing them! Hidden books about killers, handwritten murder manuals, then this whole darn grand scheme." He huffed again. "Jesus."

"The other two's plan was stupid." Sherry plucked the cigarette from Dave's fingers and took a sharp rip herself before handing it back, exhaling an equally enormous cloud. "Sloppy. They would've been found out for sure. But still—" She nodded back toward the kitchen where Charm sat inside. "Girl's a goddamn hero for stopping it."

* * *

Betts sat on the edge of the kitchen table, speaking to Charm in a low voice. "Don't sugarcoat the rest of it now just 'cause that boy's mother felt overwhelmed or whatever. That woman is owed the truth, whether or not she can handle it." Betts took a drag off her long, skinny cigarette but didn't blow out on her exhale, letting the smoke instead protrude naturally from her nose and lips, billowing upward in little white tendrils before her eyes. "You just keep telling it right, every detail."

"Yes, ma'am."

Betts gave her a wink from behind the smoke curtain. No smile, just a wink, but Charm could tell she was proud. And for an instant as fleeting as that wink, Charm desperately wanted to tell her grand-godmother what had really happened the night before. The honest version. Every detail.

Yet Charm knew she'd never be able to. Never, ever. She smashed a pumpkin over an innocent boy's head and helped tape up his unconscious body. So even though she managed to save Billy in the end, the truth of her actions before that point would surely break her grand-godmother. What Charm didn't know was how to reconcile that with herself. It put a pit in her belly, a sinking stomach feeling she feared would remain forever.

She just wanted the night to be over. For this whole event to be behind her. Then she would move on with her life and never do a bad thing ever again.

"What's wrong, child?" Betts asked.

Charm didn't know what to say, so she voiced the first thing that came to mind. "My best friend fell into evil, like yours did. My real grandmother."

Betts's face betrayed no reaction, but she swallowed hard, clearly taken aback. "You're right." And she nodded. "Heavens, you're right." She put a wrinkled, tender hand on one of Charm's. "I will tell you the story sometime. Sooner, now."

Five minutes later Officer Sherry popped back in. She walked over, stood by the table. "Charm."

Charm looked up.

"When Tildra was in the restroom with Billy, and you and Maggie-Lynn were waiting outside for her, was that your first time *alone* with Maggie-Lynn since being apart the whole summer?" Sherry asked.

Charm thought. She nodded as though only just realizing herself. "It was. Yup."

"What did y'all talk about?"

More thinking. "She asked how it was in the city. With my cousins." Charm touched her purple lip again, poking it, poking it.

2

THE FIRST NIGHT

Garbed in black sheet-robes, masks pushed up on their heads, they stood and waited just outside the entrance to the restroom like Tildra had instructed. The starlight was still more than enough to see by, but Magg lit a lantern for good measure and set it on the ground between them. It cast a yellowish glowing circle across the brick wall. Beside the far end of the building there stood another of the graveyard's yew trees. It was overgrown like the rest—very old, very wrinkled, and over the years it had started leaning over, tilting more and more after each additional year until it leaned directly into the restroom itself, fusing with the top corner of the building. Its trunk formed around that top corner like a tree-mouth enjoying a brick meal, its long twisting branches covering that end of the roof like a thicket of wild arms guarding its new food.

"Tildra wouldn't do anything in there without us, right?" Charm asked, almost with an air of fear, or longing.

"No, she won't even touch him during the first part," Magg said. "It's her pre-ritual. She's showing him a sketch she drew of him being tortured. To mess with his mind. Psychological warfare."

"Oh, okay. Sweet."

"So, how was it in the city?" Magg asked. "With your cousins?"

"Well, they were happy you didn't come this year."

Magg laughed. "I bet."

Charm said nothing.

"Look," Magg said. "I'm sorry I didn't come this summer. I know our pranks on them would have been brilliant as always—"

"You had your cheerleader tryouts and stuff, I understand. I'm thrilled you made the team. You wanted it and you earned it."

This time it was Magg who kept quiet.

"But yeah, I wanted to strangle them," Charm said. "Little shits never left me alone. I spent most of the free time I did have at the bookstore." She gave Magg a sly smile. "Stole a book on my last day too."

"Nice! What book?"

"Oh, that reminds me!" Charm exclaimed. "Something strange happened." Gooseflesh flared up her spine as she remembered. "So I was there, right? At the bookstore on my last day, waiting to see some new releases. I bought one and hid another under my sweater. That wasn't an issue. And to answer your question, the one I stole is called *How to Kill People in Space*. It's absolutely ridiculous. I love it so far. But anyhow, after I walked out of the store, this man on the sidewalk came up to me. Like, right up to me—he smelled pretty lethal. Asked if I had a quarter. I gave him one. His face was dirty. But one of his eyes . . . it was all purple and bloody, dotted with these little black spots. He looked right at me with it, his other eye closed, and said, 'Thanks, kid.

You're a *charm*. You'll be saved by the stars.' Obviously he couldn't have known my name, and I haven't a clue what he meant, but that's just bizarre, right? The whole exchange gave me the chills—actually, more than that. It creeped me out if I'm being honest. Weird, huh?"

Magg scrunched her brows, nodded, mulled it over. Then, "He was a nut," she proposed, shrugging. "Crazy'll give you the chills every time."

Charm thought on that for a second. "Not that I mind, but I don't think it's quite fair for us to judge anyone's sanity."

Magg was almost bashful. "Yeah, but you see, we *know* we're insane—and that practically makes us sane. So take pride in that we don't do this 'cause we're crazy."

"So why do we?" Charm asked.

Magg looked at her disappointed, as though the answer were obvious. "Because it's like Tildra said. We're the sadistic brats who're gonna terrify this town for the next fifty, sixty, maybe seventy years." Her face lit up with glee. "We're gonna create urban legends. Our own folklore."

Charm gave Magg a stare.

Then she burst out with laughter.

"Sorry," she said, trying and failing to stifle herself as Magg frowned. "It's just . . . is this really what we're doing with our lives? I mean, screw it, I'm in, don't get me wrong. It's just, I know we've always been into the sick and twisted, but we've never *done* anything sick and twisted before tonight. Almost makes me wonder if Tildra put a spell on us." She laughed again, halfheartedly. Magg said nothing. "Okay, look," she continued. "You know I support whatever makes you happy. But this is big, Magg, so I'm only asking 'cause my conscience demands it: Are you really sure you want to take such a long-term risk? Especially when—"

But before Charm could finish her carefully worded rant, Tildra shoved through the slow-moving, rusty hinged bathroom door and came outside with her mask pushed up. She was sweating and giddy. "I'm done with the first part. Y'all wanna come inside and see?"

"Yes," Magg said without pause, each of her sharp eyes holding a starry twinkle.

THE SECOND NIGHT

Everyone's smokes were done. Intermission was over.

Officer Sherry leaned against the counter, notepad and pen at the ready.

Betts stood in her corner, leaning against the fridge, arms crossed.

Ralph, Julia, and Detective Dave took their seats around the small table once more. Dave produced his pen, clicked it, and gave Charm a nod.

The kid took a breath. "Like I said, Tildra came outside and asked if we were ready. And that was when I found out what was really going on. They just assumed they could talk me into going along with it. But they were wrong about me."

PART III

THE SISTERHOOD OF BLOODY ARTISTS

1

THE FIRST NIGHT

As Billy sat alone in the restroom all taped up, he realized Tildra probably didn't like him back. Maybe she never liked him. After all, she did just present to him a fully detailed illustration of him having been brutally mutilated. Maybe this was her plan all along. He'd snuck out to meet her and nobody knew where he was. Now, he was at her mercy, in mortal danger (unless this was all some awful prank), and there was no breaking out of so much duct tape. They'd wrapped him up from the waist down like a purple mummy.

They came in—his captors.

Three of them, entering one by one through the door, each cloaked figure holding it open for the one behind, all wearing those black robes and sick purple masks.

Of course, there had to be three of them, he realized. Tildra, Maggie-Lynn, and whoever had hit him on the head!

They marched toward him, single file, slowly and methodically. Two of the three held a small black pillow between gloved hands. They took their places before him, standing side-by-side, presenting themselves.

The two on the right and left knelt before him, placing

their small black pillows under their knees, seemingly for comfort against the hard and dirty brick floor. The third figure in the middle remained standing, arms crossed. Billy took a closer look at their purple skull-shaped masks. He could tell they were homemade now. Probably paper mâché.

Tildra, kneeling before Billy on his left, spoke first. "Bill, William, or Billy Tippard, whichever one you truly are, we have selected you as the inaugural sacrifice in the Sisterhood of Bloody Artists." She began performing an odd movement with her arms, waving them around in a slow but continuous motion. Then she hummed a moment, light and sweet, eyes closed behind her mask.

This must be a prank, Billy thought. Or hoped, rather.

Tildra stopped and went still, then spoke again in a calm, casual tone. "Perhaps angels are waiting for you, Billy. On the other side, ready to nurse your soul and take you into paradise. Perhaps. But I like to think there are *monsters* waiting. Monsters that control everything. From the weather to our dreams to our destinies. They see all points in time and reflect on us in ways we never could about ourselves. They're not angels, but demons—like me. You see, I consider myself a demon in human form sent directly from the netherworld to cause chaos—and you're in *my* hell now. A special realm where you will be sacrificed to the true gods. Billy, none of this is a lie. You're dying tonight."

Too stunned and incredulous for words (which was just as well since he couldn't speak through duct tape anyway), Billy began to both sweat and shiver with the reality of it all. Having been knocked unconscious, kidnapped at the command of the girl he liked—her telling him they were going to kill him, and his sudden realization that he believed her, Tildra's words had the intended effect. Billy now knew without a doubt that this was real.

This was no prank. He was a fool for hoping so.

Tildra looked to her left at Maggie-Lynn, who was kneeling on Billy's right, and nodded, indicating it was Magg's turn to speak.

Beneath her mask, Magg chuckled. "Sounds like a nut, huh?" she said, facing Billy but cocking her head toward Tildra. "Like everything she just said is completely mad, right? Most folks would certainly think so. But most folks don't know the truth. You spend your whole lives thinking evil stuff happens to other people. People in stories or in faraway places, people you see on the news but never meet." She leaned forward and her voice became a loud, vicious growl. *"But now you know, William! Now you know the—"*

Billy couldn't take it. He spasmed in anger, triggered by Maggie-Lynn's snarly tone. He jerked his shoulders and rocked his head with almost no control over his actions. He was also terrified (nearly pissing himself and barely holding it), roaring a desperate hum through the duct tape over his mouth in a mix of rage and fear.

Maggie-Lynn leaned up and slapped him, hard, right across his face with her gloved hand. Fiery pain erupted in his left cheek.

It shut him up.

Magg leaned back and continued casually. "Now you know the secret truth of this world that most are willfully blind to: Monsters are real. This is really happening to you, Billy. Maybe whatever gods that do exist *are* wicked—and maybe you're just not in their favor." She pushed up her mask, regarding Billy face-to-face. She was sweating. "Or maybe, Billy, you're just really unlucky. I don't care either way. I've always wanted to know what it's like to kill someone and I've always thought you were annoying, so you're perfect." She pulled her mask back down over her face and looked up at the standing figure next to her. "Charm, you don't have to, but do you wanna say something?"

Charm stood there, arms crossed. She took a deep breath, muffled by her mask. Then she pushed her mask up.

Billy heard Charm's name called but was astonished to see it really was her. He'd known Charm since first grade, had visited her house for birthday and Halloween parties with half their class. She'd been to his home for the same. True, he'd known Maggie-Lynn just as long as he'd known Charm, but Billy always felt Magg hadn't liked him—and he'd never once been invited to her house. But Charm—even if they were never that close—had always been kind to him. Always.

"Look," Charm said to him. "I'm as surprised as you. This whole thing. I mean, yes, Magg and I, we've talked about it over the years—what it'd be like to end a life. What our serial killer names would be . . ." She chuckled uneasily. "But it was always pretend. I never thought we'd actual-ly . . ." She shrugged, as if unable to think of what else to say. But she held up a gloved finger, looking frustrated with herself, indicating for him to wait. Then, nodding, she said, "I know you got, like, human rights and everything. Sorry I'm not sorry, Billy."

Magg and Tildra watched her. They nodded as well, in approval under their masks, letting Charm know she was doing a good job.

Charm was done. She pulled the mask back down over her face.

Tildra looked at Billy and wondered aloud, "Does he have any last words?"

"I wanna hear what he has to say," Magg answered.

Billy began to silently weep. Tildra reached forward,

grabbing a tip of the purple duct tape across his mouth with two gloved fingers.

She let go and laughed through her mask. "Just kidding."

"Just kidding," Magg reiterated.

"Just messin'," Tildra said.

"Just messin'," Magg repeated. "Your last words will forever be—" She raised her arms in mock-fright and gave another absolutely awful impression of him in that high, uneven voice, "'*What's goin' on?*'"

Bound in duct tape, plastered in pumpkin guts, Billy felt bamboozled and exhausted. His hair was sweat-stuck to his numb and tender head, and his cheek was also now sore where Maggie-Lynn had slapped him. He didn't want to give up, but he didn't want to get smacked again either. He was thoroughly beaten down, in both a figurative and literal sense.

Tildra leaned forward again and placed a hand on Billy's knee. "We'll return promptly. But we must first privately discuss how to make the most of your misery."

She finger-tapped Billy on the nose and stood up, Maggie-Lynn following suit, picking the little black pillows up off the ground with them. With Charm in tow and Tildra leading the way, the three girls in their robes and masks slowly marched in single file toward the door.

Until Tildra abruptly stopped and turned around, causing Magg to bump into her.

"Sorry!"

Tildra ignored her. "Damn it. I forgot we need the bag."

"I got it!" Magg handed Charm the two pillows and dashed across the dirty floor, holding up the knees of her sheet-robe so she wouldn't trip on herself. She grabbed the purple duffel bag with red and black stars all over it and trotted back half as fast to her spot in line between Charm and Tildra.

Billy watched them leave the restroom, each cloaked figure holding the door open for the one behind as they exited.

2

Tildra cut around the knives inside the plastic packaging with Maggie-Lynn's red scissors. They stood outside the restroom entrance, lantern still placed on the ground from earlier. Tildra dropped the scissors into the duffel bag and ripped the packaging open. All three girls had their masks pushed up on top of their sweaty heads. They were also a little pale, a little dehydrated, and maybe just a little out of their minds.

Tildra held up the open knife set. "So, who wants what and how are we doing this?"

"Wow," Charm said. "I'm surprised y'all haven't had this part figured out the most."

"Oh, we exchanged many different ideas," Magg said. "So many. But in the end . . ." She shrugged. "Just told ourselves we'd figure it out when the time came."

"Can't believe that," Charm mused.

"It is part of the fun, though," Tildra said. She removed all three blades and dropped the packaging back into the purple duffel bag. She spread the knives out in both of her gloved hands: the big hunting knife, the serrated knife, and the little pocketknife. "I need the big one," she said, almost to herself, staring down at the largest of the three blades with a starlit shine in her eyes. "I have plans with this."

"Which one you want, Charm?" Magg asked. "I don't care."

"I guess the pocketknife would be cool," Charm said. "Stick him half a dozen times and watch his face." She lifted her right hand, holding an imaginary pocketknife, and performed half a dozen lightning-fast air stabs.

Tildra looked impressed and handed Charm the real pocketknife. Charm pulled out the little blade—as one does to make sure it works and to satisfy curiosity—then pushed it back in. She pulled up one side of the black sheet she was wearing and tucked the pocketknife into her jeans pocket. Maggie-Lynn took the jagged, serrated knife.

Tildra caressed the big knife with her gloved fingers. "Thing is," she muttered, "what'd really be satisfying for me would be to just—" She suddenly stabbed the air in front of her with one arm in a big SWOOSH, a formidable show of quickness and strength. "Stab him right in the face like how the Benders did it. If only."

"But then it would be over," Magg said matter-of-factly.

Tildra lowered the knife. "But then it would be over. And that's no fun."

"We gotta make it last," Magg said.

"We have to," Tildra concurred, but still bit her lip, looking at the ground. "All this trouble we went through, we have to. And I don't want him passing out neither, so we can't start with cutting off his nose or his toes or anything else too extreme." She glanced at the serrated knife in Magg's hand. "Consequently, I don't know if we should really use the saw-type knife. It's too jagged."

"Do you wanna torture him or not?" Magg teased, a

playful smile on her face. "What's with the G-rated approach all of a sudden?"

Charm laughed at that and crossed her arms, watching them both with curious, childish wonder, as though this were her favorite part of the night so far. As though she had a front-row seat to the greatest show on Earth.

"Shut up," Tildra said with her own little smirk, shaking her head.

Magg went on. "Once he's used to some poking, *accepts* some poking, he'll be ready to have a finger amputated."

Charm touched her nose, poked it over and over. "It actually would be kinda neat to see someone's nose get sawed off. Shoot, that'd be wild."

"I'm not fully opposed to something like that," Tildra clarified. "But we gotta work up to it. That's a final-act kind of thing. I know I was the one who said I wanted to stab him in the face and all, but thinking responsibly, it's important that we cherish this memory and take our time." She made eye contact with them both, making sure they heard her. "This is a fun and wonderful moment of course, but let's not indulge ourselves too quickly."

"I wouldn't mind strangling him a little bit," Charm announced. "Let go, then choke again. A back-and-forth sort of thing. Stop right before he passes out."

Magg gave her a wide-eyed look, and Charm knew why. It was because years ago she'd told Magg that if she ever were to kill for fun, it would be to strangle the life out of somebody. Charm winked in response.

"Okay, but first we'll start him out with something mild," Magg said. "Maybe your pocketknife? For some poking?"

"That's fine." Charm trailed off from their conversation just then, suddenly staring at the giant tree looming large at the end corner of the restroom, conjoined with the top of the building. She noticed the old trunk had what looked like countless years' worth of carvings all over it from visitors throughout the decades, perhaps even centuries, and it triggered a realization.

"This is the tree," Charm said.

Maggie-Lynn looked at her, then over at the tree, then back at Charm. She closed her eyes and laughed. A little too hard for Charm's liking.

"Is it?" Tildra asked. "The one Maggie-Lynn jumped out of to scare you?"

"It is," Magg answered, still guffawing. Then, to Charm, "I thought you knew that this whole time. You only just realized?"

Charm glanced up at the restroom roof, where the branches covered one corner. She walked to the tree and placed a hand on the trunk. "I wish we could carve our names into it," she said. "But that probably wouldn't be wise."

Tildra joined Charm beside the tree and also put a hand on it, running her black-gloved fingers over the different carvings. She proposed an alternative: "What if we carve the letters S. B. A. for Sisterhood of Bloody Artists?"

"Or . . ." Magg came toward them, wearing a mad grin under her sharp, wide eyes as she held up the serrated knife. "We could carve S. B. A. into Billy's forehead."

"That's a little too heavy-handed," Tildra said apprehensively, but in good nature. "I'd like to be more subtle."

"Well . . ." Magg tried to think, undeterred. "We could—"

"I need to pee," Charm said.

"Use the boys' side," Tildra said.

"Sure." Billy was taped up and trapped in the girls' section, so it made sense for Charm to use the side that wasn't occupied.

Magg carried on as Charm marched off. "What we could do is cut him up all over and just carve a tiny little S in one spot and then a B in another and then an A . . ." Her voice drifted away.

The boys' side was a mirrored identical to the girls' in its layout, only this side also had old urinals lined along the wall next to the sinks. After pushing through the door and stepping in, Charm stood suspended in a starlight beam blasting through the bare window on the far wall.

"Let's see who's scary now," she whispered to herself.

Charm strode across the dirt-caked brick floor toward that window on the far side. She took her mask off and placed it down on the last sink next to the wall. She hopped up on the sink and climbed into the window.

"See who's scary when I fall from the branches on top of *you*," she muttered under her breath, unaware she'd even spoken aloud. She easily slipped outside through the window and climbed upward, hoisting herself up onto the roof. Charm giggled in excitement. She still didn't know how she was going to manage the rest of the night and what she'd have to do, but she knew she had to do *this* right now while the moment was opportune.

She held up the knees of her sheet-robe and tiptoed across the flat roof of the restroom, staying low and careful not to crunch any fallen leaves. When she got near the tree-corner, she peeked over the side and saw Tildra still standing beside the trunk, Magg right next to her. They were talking.

Charm smiled. Her idea had worked perfectly. The reason she had walked over and put her hand on the tree in the first place was in the hope that Magg would come stand beside it as well.

She crouched lower when she reached the branches,

those long ancient arms stretching over the roof. Charm softly placed her left foot on one thick branch, pushing down with her weight to make sure it was sturdy. She then grabbed with her left hand a higher branch (less thick, less sturdy) just as she began hearing Maggie-Lynn and Tildra speaking in hushed voices.

"I just wish she woulda brought the darn Bender book," Tildra was saying, sounding disappointed, almost whiny. "That's the only thing. Now I'll never get to read it."

"Nah, we can get another copy at a bookstore somewhere," Magg replied. "I know which book it is. Might be a little hard to find, but—"

"I know that. I wanted to read *hers*."

"Ahhh, I see. Yeah, you gotta make peace with that never happening."

Charm frowned, staring down at her two supposed comrades, listening now. She knelt a little lower, removing her left hand from the branch it held.

"Having *her* Bender book after we kill her would've meant everything to me," Tildra said, sounding emotional now—which she must've been because her voice broke. "*It could have made this whole thing a masterp—*"

"Ssshhh," Magg shushed.

Tildra brought it down. "I can't believe she was actually forgetful enough to forget it after you just reminded her today. What an oblivious idiot."

Charm's brain was still processing what her ears were hearing.

Magg squealed, "I can't wait to see the look on her face when you put a knife in it!"

"Sssshhhh." This time it was Tildra's turn to shush. "But yeah, Bender-style!" she said, and stabbed the air again with her big knife.

3

THREE WEEKS BEFORE THE VIOLENT NIGHTS

10:16 P.M.

Maggie-Lynn and Tildra were drunk and tired, hanging out in Tildra's room. Tildra lay on her bed, which happened to be nothing more than a flimsy mattress on the floor. She couldn't care less, though. She was comfortable as could be with her hands folded across her tummy, eyes closed, a smile on her face. Her horn-rimmed glasses were just hanging off her nose and ear.

The wallpaper in her room had peeled, revealing cracks in the wood that were shaped like lightning. A poster of Alfred Hitchcock's 1948 film *Rope* was pinned on the bedroom door. Slumped in a red beanbag at the foot of Tildra's bed, Magg held a 750 mL glass bottle, stolen from her parents' cabinet. The label on the bottle read "Whiskey of the Fox." It was still mostly full—the girls were light-weights, naturally. Piled up around the carpet were stacks of books and folders and journals. Tildra's folders and journals. Years' worth of them. Cluttered yet organized. In the corner sat a black duffel bag with cans of red and purple paint next to it. The only light in the room was the single, dim bulb hanging from the center of the ceiling.

Maggie-Lynn didn't know if Tildra was asleep or not. With her vision slightly blurred, she gazed around the room for a while, losing herself in thought.

"Honestly," she finally thought out loud. "No, never mind."

Tildra simply nodded in reply, her eyes remaining shut, her slight smile staying at attention. Magg, looking at the wall, didn't notice.

"It's just—" And then Magg let it all out in a drunken, long-buried rant. It wasn't a full-blown tirade, but her feelings were hurt. It was only her second time drinking, and the liquor gave her the courage to finally admit what she felt out loud. "She'd rather go to the city over summer without me than stay here and try out for Cheer with me—even though she hates her cousins! And she didn't even consider how that makes me feel. Just totally dismissed it when I asked her to try out with me. Why couldn't she at least think about it? Why couldn't she just do it? I wanted us to infiltrate the cool kids, and—well, that's a whole different thing. A separate thing. But—what was I . . . ? Oh, yeah. I wish she could've just been there for me. I usually go with her to the city every summer, you know. And the one year I ask us to stay home for something I want, she flakes. And she's not *that* stupid; she could've at least known that her saying no might hurt my feelings. But I bet that didn't even occur to her. She doesn't care. She's like my sister, but she doesn't love me back. I bet she doesn't even know she doesn't love me. She's always been that way too. Indifferent-like. Not caring what anyone thinks or says or does or feels. It's like she's dead inside."

Keeping her eyes closed and not moving anything other than her arm, Tildra raised her right hand like a kid in class and chimed in with a suggestion. "We could kill her when we kill Billy."

Maggie-Lynn jerked her head around so hard that her neck would be sore for a week. She stared at Tildra for a long time, stunned.

4

———

TWO WEEKS BEFORE THE VIOLENT NIGHTS

8:55 P.M.

In Maggie-Lynn's room, the framed photo on the wall of her and Charm was (for now) gone. Instead, a picture of Magg and Tildra sitting on the floor together had been placed in a new frame and set on the bedside table beside the boombox. As part of the act, these photos would be switched back just before Charm returned from the city.

It was a sleepover, Magg and Tildra both in their pajamas. Magg lazed on her side on the shaggy red carpet, resting her head on one arm. A few stuffed animals dotted the floor around her: a bunny, a fox, an owl. Tildra stood, performing a slow, fluid dance—almost ceremonial—to one of her mixtapes of soothing, dark classical-style music playing from the boombox. Magg didn't recognize the melody but would soon be swaying her head to it.

Tildra pushed her glasses back up as she danced. "We'd be darkists: dark artists."

"Hmmm. Darkists of the Sisterhood," Magg said, seeing how it sounded. She smiled. "I like that."

"I made it up."

"I know."

"If we can bag Charm," Tildra said while executing a slow twirl, "it would elevate what we're planning to more than just ritual murder. It'd make the whole piece something with real complexity, with depth. Like Shakespeare—only we're serial killers."

"Totally," Magg said from the carpet. "I get it. Performative theater, elaborate betrayals, *death*. A true test of the arts—especially if we do like you suggested and let her pick one of the knives to hold as part of the trick, part of the act."

After nodding in agreement, Tildra suddenly bent her knees and dipped down, throwing her arms out and busting some sort of bizarre dance move. She held the pose for several seconds before coming up again and settling back into the slow groove of her strange music.

5

ONE WEEK BEFORE THE VIOLENT NIGHTS

11:28 A.M.

Hunched in hushed conversation, Maggie-Lynn and Tildra sat across from each other at one of the long reading tables inside the dimly lit library where sunlight never penetrated. They were almost nose to nose. They were also the only two people in the library, but their silence was practical. Better safe than sorry. They were discussing "top secret matters," after all.

"We could make it look like Charm and Billy killed each other," Magg said. "Or we could make it look like they were both killed by someone el—"

"What do we do if she's not down to kill Billy with us?" Tildra asked. "What if she says no when we ask her?"

"She'll say yes—and if she doesn't, then we kill her on the spot. Right there in my room."

"*What if your parents hear?!*"

"That's the point. We'll say she attacked us. That she was jealous of our friendship and had a breakdown. And then we just reschedule Billy. No biggie."

Tildra stared at her, blinking.

"She'll say yes," Magg said.

"Are you one-hundred percent sure that we can outsmart this girl? Our pitch to convince her that we'll all get away with it is a bit thin . . ."

"I am." Magg laughed. "I definitely am. The only thing holding Charm back from seeing right through us is her not caring enough to pay any real attention."

"That's, well, not very reassuring, to be honest."

Maggie-Lynn laughed again at any threat Charm might pose. "I'm just being dramatic. Trust me, I know her. The last thing she'll do is see it coming."

"You sure you want me to do this? Kill your best friend?"

"*You're* my best friend," Magg said.

"But you're sure you want *me* to do it? Not you?"

"I'll feel more powerful if I witness you do it," Magg admitted. "I wanna *watch* it happen."

Tildra regarded her, straight-faced. Then she began to smirk, looking pleased. "You're ruthless."

"And you ain't?"

Tildra ignored the rebuttal. "We have to do it Bender-style. It's gotta be quick—I won't underestimate her. I'm stabbing her right in the face."

6

———

THE FIRST NIGHT

Stuck like a statue up on the restroom roof, Charm was in a state of utter disbelief—the beaming, thumping, pulsing stars of the Milky Way shining bright as ever through the branches above her. Maggie-Lynn and Tildra continued to laugh and mumble down below, their voices floating up to the roof and drifting into Charm's ears.

"Yeah, screw her," Magg was saying. "It's what she gets. It ain't only 'cause she wouldn't do Cheer with me. I've realized a lot. She'll never care much about the cult or our work. For her, all this stuff is just something to do. She is so weird."

As Charm blinked a few times in surprise, a quick bolt of long, crooked lightning struck down silently in the far-off distance ahead of her. She didn't even notice it.

"When we go back inside, I'm gonna ask Billy if he wants to *see something*," Tildra said in a loud whisper. She held up the big knife. "That's when I'm gonna get her. So, if you wanna say anything to Charm, you know, cryptic-like, parting words or whatever, do it soon."

Maggie-Lynn was nodding. Meanwhile, Charm slowly lifted her left foot off the branch to begin backing away.

"Hey, so," Tildra said, "what *were* yours and Charm's serial killer names?"

"Hold that thought. I need to pee too."

"Sure, me three."

Charm almost tripped in her haste and terror as she turned, rapidly tiptoeing her way back across the roof. She got down, leaned over the edge, lowered her legs into the window and crawled back inside the boys' restroom, heart racing.

She was about halfway through the window when Magg and Tildra walked in on her, their knives still in their hands. Charm dropped to the floor.

Magg and Tildra looked confused. Nervous, even—their unsure, matching expressions marked with lines of worry.

Charm played it off. "Oh, shoot!" She laughed, acting embarrassed.

"What were you doing?" Tildra asked.

Charm kept it cool. "I was gonna try to scare you—scare Maggie-Lynn. But y'all caught me. Darn it! I was gonna try to climb up on the roof and get in the tree and jump out of it to scare y'all, or maybe just jump off the roof. Hadn't really figured it out yet."

Magg and Tildra gave each other a look as if speaking without words. Then Magg cackled as she turned her head back to Charm. "Sorry to ruin your revenge."

"I really wanted to get you," Charm said, trying to sound both casual and frustrated.

Tildra smiled. "Well, you'll always have tomorrow."

Charm looked at Tildra—perhaps a little too long— before releasing a chuckle and shaking her head. She was vaguely aware Magg had started speaking about Billy again, but her mind was too busy, wrapped and warped and stunned by what she'd learned while eavesdropping. The knowledge of the impending attack against her by the two maniacs she was with was so surreal to her that it felt unreal, and she was trying her best to stay present and focused and not fall into a dream-like trance, lamenting her friendship with Magg, wishing it hadn't gone wrong. *"Instead of trying to plan the torture out,"* Magg was saying somewhere in the background, *"how about we just go in there and see what happens? We just have to promise ourselves we won't get carried away . . ."*

7

Charm sat at her tiny kitchen table in the dark, the only light being that of the stars coming in through the window over the sink. It was hours after the events at the graveyard. Her hair was down—released from its bun—and she wore the sweater, blue jeans, and sneakers she'd had on underneath the black sheet-robe, now long discarded.

She was covered in dried-up blood—all over her face and clothes, though none of it was her own. Her lip was busted and swollen purple.

"I didn't have a choice," she said.

Ralph was in his pajamas, hair disheveled and wide-eyed, looking bewildered. He sat next to his daughter, facing her.

Betts stood by the table in a nightgown and had a large, hand-carved wooden cross around her neck, her right hand wrapped tightly around it. In her free hand was Charm's fox glass filled up with grape punch. She handed the glass to Charm, who took it gratefully.

"You're my kid," Ralph said. "Toughest kid I ever known. I can't even begin to explain how—how proud I am. It's important for you to know that right now. You can rest easy, baby darlin'. You did the right thing. Ain't nothing gonna happen to you."

"We should probably call the cops now," Charm said. She began gulping down the grape drink.

"I'll call Detective Dave," her father said. "We've played poker before."

8

THE SECOND NIGHT

"When Magg and I followed Tildra into the bathroom, I was overwhelmed with guilt seeing Billy." Charm shuddered at the kitchen table. "Tildra had somehow knocked him out, had him all taped up so he couldn't move. That's when they told me about the plan to kill him. That's when Tildra pulled out the robes, offered me a mask, and said we were gonna start a secret killing club. They told me I didn't have to join or do any part in it. Maggie-Lynn just wanted me to be there, to witness the whole thing. They just assumed I'd go along with it. I told them we couldn't. That while pranking him was funny, he definitely didn't deserve to be killed. And they found out real quick that they shouldn't have invited me. They weren't gonna let me free Billy, so—"

"I'm sorry, hon," Officer Sherry butted in. "Could you back it up and slow it down for a minute. We need some more details."

"Oh, sure. Yes, ma'am," Charm said, cooperating.

Everyone else in the room rolled their eyes and even groaned.

"Hold on, now," Julia tried to interject.

"You can always go back and get details later," Ralph said to Sherry. "Just let her tell it how she's telling it."

Detective Dave seemed to agree with Ralph. "Go ahead," he said to Charm.

Sherry frowned, and for the first and only time that night she wrote something down on her little notepad.

"Well, I told them I was taking Billy, and they told me no, I wasn't," Charm continued. "They told me they had knives. And I tried talking to Magg. Just her. Tildra didn't like that, and I guess that's when they decided they weren't gonna let me leave either. Looking back on it, I think that was their plan the whole time—either I do it with them, or they do me in along with Billy. Just depended on how I reacted, I guess. And they didn't like my reaction, so Tildra tried to stick me with a pocketknife."

Julia gasped. "Jesus Christ."

"But then I took it from her," Charm went on. "So *I* had the pocketknife. And Magg didn't like that very much." Charm mused for a moment, lowering her eyes. She huffed air out of her nostrils. "Magg was mad at me for not doing cheerleading training with her at summer school, and that caught me off guard. I didn't even know. Honestly." Charm bowed her head.

"Go on," Detective Dave nudged her.

"Do you need a minute?" Julia asked.

"No, I'm . . ." Charm tried to say, her voice cracking. "It's just . . ."

"It's okay," Julia said softly.

Ralph gently patted his daughter's back.

Charm sighed. "No, it's just, they *attacked* me. I had the pocketknife, but then they each pulled out a bigger knife—my best friend and her little monster—and that's when the whole world changed. It felt like I was in ancient times." She looked up and around at them all. "Like I was fighting in a battle."

In some way, Ralph and Betts couldn't have looked prouder of Charm, but they were also visibly heartbroken for her at the same time. Brows twitching, jaws clenched, the both of them. Their eyes full of pride, their faces full of sorrow.

Officer Sherry tapped her pen back and forth on her notepad, over and over and over again, incessantly. She did so because she was zoned out, squinting in deep thought.

"I thought me dying was real in that moment," Charm said, telling the story. "I thought for sure I was gonna at least get stabbed." She poked her bruised lip again.

Across Sherry's notepad was written one simple sentence in a barely legible scrawl:

girl's a goddamn liar

PART IV

A VIOLENT NIGHT

1

———

THE FIRST NIGHT

Maggie-Lynn, Tildra, and Charm came out of the boys' restroom.

Tildra picked up the duffel bag by its straps with one hand. "Let's go. Masks on."

"Oh, I left mine on the sink!" Charm blurted. "One second!"

She pushed through the door and darted back inside, all the way down to the last sink along the wall where she'd left her mask, next to that big square hole which made a window. Charm picked up the mask, examining it, pondering her predicament. Outside the window a dazzling, bright purple shooting star blasted across the night sky like a space bullet, leaving a streak of violet in its wake that slowly dissipated.

Charm didn't notice. She went back out and rejoined the other two.

Magg and Tildra still had their knives drawn, ready to go. With all three wearing their masks, sheet-robes, and black leather gloves, Tildra led the way into the girls' restroom for the final time, pushing open the creaking door.

Inside, Billy was fighting to free himself (still to no avail, barely able to budge) but went motionless as soon as the trio came in. Tildra set down the duffel bag with a laugh and waved away any worries. "No harm, no foul," she said to him. "I won't hold it against you—can't expect you not to try. Though, I'm surprised you still got any circulation, honestly." Tildra cackled, turning to her cohorts with a half-twirl as she tilted her masked head to the side. "You know, I'm finally starting to feel pretty villainous."

"All hail the demon queen," Maggie-Lynn said playfully.

Charm nodded fast and hard in agreement underneath her own paper mâché visage. She was so nervous that she was afraid to even swallow, for fear the click in her throat would be too loud.

"Only next time we'll *look* like royalty," Tildra said. "These rags served their purpose well for our first time, but they still look like cheap sheets."

"Oh," Magg let out, and Charm could tell she was hurt by the remark. "It's just . . . they were the only black sheets that we had . . ."

"It's okay," Tildra said. "Trial-and-error is to be expected. We'll just steal some nice sheets next time. Until we manage to get real robes. With hoods!" Her eyes lit up behind her mask at the thought.

Billy watched this conversation taking place in front of him in what seemed like frozen, terrified awe. Charm stared right at him. She would do Billy no further harm, but perhaps she could pretend otherwise to buy some time. Perhaps, with some luck, she could somehow cut him free with her pocketknife before the other two intervened. "So, um, is it okay if I stand him up and choke him for a little bit? Maybe let me put on a show for you guys?"

"Charm, I actually have an anecdote for you before we begin," Magg said.

Tildra looked down at Billy. "The funny thing about the future, William, is that it always happens in the present." She face-palmed her mask, frustrated with herself. "Man, I really need to work on my cringey dialogue." She threw out her arms and bent her knees, dipping down into another one of her ritualistic dance moves.

Magg put her hand on Charm's shoulder and said, "Do you remember before Halloween last year when—"

"Magg." Charm cut her off in a low voice so Tildra wouldn't make out the words. "I think you're overreacting about me not wanting to try out for cheerleading."

Magg's eyes expanded behind her skull mask. Charm, thinking on her feet, turned and quickly strode toward Billy and Tildra. She pulled up one side of her black sheet, taking the pocketknife from her jeans pocket and pulling out the little blade, setting it between the middle and ring fingers of her gloved right hand like a spike and making a fist. She pulled off her mask with her free hand and dropped it to the floor.

"Hey, Billy," Charm said. "You wanna *see* something?"

Charm turned to Tildra and put her free hand on the shorter girl's shoulder. With her other hand—her spiked fist—Charm began punching Tildra in the gut, over and over and over again.

Magg pulled off her own mask, her expression stunned, as if unable to comprehend what she was seeing.

Billy, eyes shocked, seemingly couldn't believe the sight either.

After seven swift strikes to the stomach, Charm let go and stepped back, her spiked fist painted in red.

Tildra turned to Maggie-Lynn, holding her bloody gut, and coughed out the obvious. "*I think she knows.*"

Tildra fell to the floor.

Magg dropped her mask. It clattered on the ground. Her lips and jaw were twitching. "Tildra?" she asked, faint hope in her voice.

Tildra whimpered in pain under her own purple skull mask, still clutching her red belly as she lay in the fetal position.

"You were my best friend, Magg," Charm said. She was stoic now. "I loved you. I just didn't wanna be a doggone cheerleader. I've no interest in it, and you knew that. But I didn't object when you decided to try out. I supported you, always did. Doesn't mean we would've grown apart. There's lots o' friends that have different hobbies and stuff."

"Do you think she's gonna die?" Magg asked, still looking at Tildra.

"Yep. I sure do."

Maggie-Lynn was pale-faced. "She might not be dying! It's just a pocketknife—"

"She's not going to survive."

"How do you know!?" Magg demanded, enraged, tears flowing out of her eyes. "It's just a tiny pocketknife!"

"Because I plan to choke the life out of her and then let Billy go. I changed my mind. I think I'm gonna be a hero."

Billy's eyes flew wide open. He jerked his head up and down.

"I'm going to kill you!" Maggie-Lynn cried.

Charm held up a finger. "You know, I'm also gonna add that I think Tildra was right about these sheets." She took off her own black sheet, removing it over her head with one arm, then held it up to look at it. "Rags," she said simply. "You even forgot to cut armholes at first. You're no artist."

Caught in the adrenaline, Charm had forgotten about the serrated knife that Maggie-Lynn still held. Magg raised the knife and lunged at Charm.

After a surge of shock that passed just as quickly as it came, Charm threw the black sheet over Magg's arm and head, forcing Magg to stop and pull the sheet off of herself as fast as she could.

It was Charm's turn to lunge forward, which she did, pocketknife still in her fist.

From the floor, Tildra suddenly grabbed Charm's leg and she tripped, falling to the ground next to the bloodied, masked demon queen.

Tildra weakly tried to lift her knife—the big knife—but Charm kicked her in the stomach. Tildra screamed in high-pitched, hellish agony.

Maggie-Lynn unleashed a battle cry—a death roar—and dropped to her knees, bringing down the serrated knife as hard as she could with both hands, aiming right for Charm's chest.

Charm dropped the pocketknife and grabbed the purple duffel bag with red and black stars all over it, pulling it over her as a shield.

Saved by the stars, she thought absurdly.

Magg buried the serrated knife into the duffel bag and its contents. Charm picked up the pocketknife, reclaiming it, and stabbed Magg in the side, just below the ribs.

Billy cheered Charm on, humming a whooping sound through the duct tape over his mouth.

Maggie-Lynn screamed, and Charm managed another quite amazing feat under the circumstances—she pulled the pocketknife out of Magg's side, kept it in her grasp, then pushed both the duffel bag and Magg off of herself. She sat up.

Weak, Tildra again tried lifting her large blade, hands shaking around the handle, slowly hoisting the big knife as if it weighed a thousand pounds. Charm turned around on the dirty brick floor and hit Tildra square in the face with the pocketknife, Bender-style, stabbing right through the paper mâché mask. Tildra didn't scream again. She just went still.

Charm let Tildra keep the pocketknife, instead taking the big knife from Tildra's now-relenting grasp. She got to her feet and turned around.

Maggie-Lynn slapped the crap out of her—right across the mouth, breaking the left side of her lower lip, which she felt rupture in searing hot pain. Magg was holding the stab wound above her hip with her other hand, leaning over, breathing heavy.

Charm's head had been knocked to the side by the slap, and she kept it there for a moment, licking her now bruised and swelling lip—as one does out of instinct when it's just been busted to hell and back.

Maggie-Lynn stared at her with hateful eyes and viciously bared teeth. But it was for show. Charm could tell it was taking every bit of Magg's strength just for her to stay standing up—one hand covering the wound on her side as she tried and failed to lessen the bleeding. A red stream gushed through the dam of her fingers.

The sight took hold of Charm, and she gaped at Magg's wound, ignoring everything else. Images of the past with her best friend rushed through her mind in flash-jolts. Sleepovers, Halloweens, vacations, all playing like an encore reel, the deeper part of her realizing there would be no more memories to add.

Magg, bleeding out and with nothing to lose, lunged for Charm's arm that held the big knife.

Charm reacted almost involuntarily, putting the big hunting knife right through Magg's throat with one fast motion, one quick strike.

Magg's hands went to her neck and the knife stuck in it. Blood splashed from her mouth and squirted between her fingers, splattering Charm's face. The geyser on Magg's side spurted freely now, streaming out across the room like a scarlet sprinkler.

Maggie-Lynn McMillan staggered back, lurching side to side, then stumbled a bit more in her delirium before turning around and crashing through one of the hanging stall doors and falling face-first into an old rusty toilet, where she died giving herself a swirly, her blood seeping everywhere.

Charm turned to Billy. "Be with you in just a moment."

She went to Tildra, who was still motionless on her back, now muttering unintelligible gibberish beneath her pierced mask.

Charm removed her black leather gloves—one now a red glove—pulling them off finger by finger, discarding them on the floor. She leaned down and sat on Tildra, pinning down the girl's arms underneath her knees in a straddle.

She took off Tildra's mask (she actually had to *tug* it off using both hands due to the pocketknife being buried so deep in her nose) and a flood of blood and tears rushed down both sides of her face. The stab wound was critical, her red snout nearly split in half. Blood pooled and swirled around her head. The air was metallic.

"Some of them have tentacles made of lightning," Tildra whispered, and Charm could tell that her wide, stricken eyes—which were aimed at the ceiling—weren't staring at anything in this realm. More like she was looking past the plane of their existence and seeing right into the next dimension. "Great purple monsters with red and black teeth. Oh yeah, they're gonna eat me. I failed to prove myself. Wasn't worthy, you see. So they'll be eating me."

Charm laughed at her. "You got real imagination. I'll admit I'm envious o' that."

She put her bare hands around Tildra's throat.

Tildra began kicking her feet.

"You wanna know what I think happened to the Bloody Benders?" Charm said, squeezing. "Legend goes the locals found out it was them who killed their relatives all along, right? And the Benders got wind and disappeared. Escaped and got away with it, right? Well, maybe they did. Maybe. But I don't think so. Get real. I bet the locals killed them. Stabbed 'em in their faces and bashed their brains in. Then buried 'em all in one unmarked grave, as a family. And the locals kept it quiet. Frontier justice. Just my theory, though."

Billy sat there taped up against the wall with his sweat and fear and dried-up pumpkin guts, witnessing the final moments of the violent battle. It took quite a while. Charm paused a few times.

* * *

Outside the restroom, there was a secret carving on the giant old yew tree that had fused itself to the roof. It was toward the bottom of the trunk on the side that faced away from the restroom—one carving in particular, hidden well among the hundreds of others.

A carving done by Tildra a week earlier:

S. B. A.

And underneath those three letters was a carved heart, also done by Tildra (for whom the risk factor really had been part of the fun, part of the act). And inside that heart, representing the intended inaugural sacrifices in the Sisterhood of Bloody Artists:

$$C + B$$

2

JUST BEFORE THE SECOND NIGHT

The sun's auburn rays streamed in through the single window of a fancy little sitting room in Billy Tippard's house. It was the type of sitting room one was usually forbidden from sitting in, unless of course there was a detective over interviewing the house's only child about their recent assault and kidnapping.

"So what happened next?" Detective Dave asked as he listened to Billy's story, just over an hour before he would set foot in Charm's kitchen.

Not counting lunch and coffee breaks, the Tippard household was Dave's fourth stop of the day so far.

He'd come to Billy's from Tildra Smith's house, and to there from Maggie-Lynn McMillan's—all after first visiting the crime scene. He'd been efficient and expedient: informing the perpetrators' families, asking quick questions, searching the perpetrators' bedrooms. The McMillan parents immediately broke down in hysterical sobs and remained that way the entire time he was there, which wasn't too long, considering. Tildra Smith's parents, on the other hand, showed almost no reaction. They sat on the couch and went into a sort of catatonic trance, taking turns staring at the wall and each other. This left Detective Dave with the house more or less to himself while he searched Tildra's bedroom. The Smiths didn't speak again while he was there. Dave departed with a nod.

Now, he sat across from Billy, his open portfolio on his lap, an ornate wooden coffee table between them. Placed all around the little room were more than a dozen antique porcelain rabbits. All different molds and sculpts. Mrs. Tippard's favorite animal, Dave might've guessed. A violet tea set with white bunnies hand-painted on the teacups sat atop a small stand underneath the shining sunlit window.

Billy looked like he'd cleaned up and gotten at least a couple hours of sleep since the previous night. However, he had a gaunt look about him, and his left cheek was bright red.

Detective Dave gently prompted him along. "Went to the old graveyard, right? To meet the girl you liked?"

"She can burn in hell," Billy said.

Dave regarded him. Billy was traumatized for sure, fidgeting one second, dead still the next. This second, he was staring hard at the coffee table, seemingly engrossed in a storm of turbulent thoughts, brooding. And like all brooders, he looked unsure of something.

"I can't even imagine what you're going through, son—"

"I got hit on the head," Billy said. "All I remember is waking up all taped up, watching Charm fight off Maggie-Lynn and Tildra. They were both trying to stab her."

"We understand that Charmane, she saved your life?" Dave had received a call from Ralph Wilson in the middle of the night, providing a short version of the events on Charm's behalf, backed up by Mrs. Tippard on Billy's behalf when she called the precinct a half-hour later.

Billy zoned out for a short moment. "Well, yeah," he finally said and nodded. "She did do that. No doubt."

"So these other two girls were planning to kill you. And she stopped them."

"They were gonna kill me for sure."

"Finish what exactly happened. The whole story. Before you got hit on the head."

"I get to the cemetery and go up to where Tildra said to meet her. And she was acting weird, talking about, I don't know, hamsters and monsters and just all-around nonsense. And then Maggie-Lynn was there. She was making fun of me, shining a flashlight in my face. I couldn't see. And then I got hit on the head with what must've been a pumpkin—I had the guts and seeds all on me. But I don't really know what happened."

"Do you know what the deal was with those purple masks and cut-up bedsheets?" Dave immediately followed up. "Stuff was strewn all over the bathroom floor."

Billy took his time, looking fidgety again. "Something about it being a ritual killing that they were planning. Charm said Tildra had wanted to kill me for a while. And I guess Charm got tricked into it, thinking it was all a prank. At the end, Charm cut me free and told me everything. But like I told my mom, I forgot all what she said. I'm sorry. Whole night was just a lot, you know. It's a blur."

3

———————

THE FIRST NIGHT

Charm, covered in Magg and Tildra's blood—which was beginning to dry up and crust on her clothes—shuffled through the purple duffel bag on the restroom floor, searching for something.

Billy was still taped up.

She wanted to free him right away but first needed to find the red scissors.

Her fingers hurt. They were sore, tired, worn-out.

She finally found the red scissors to cut Billy free. And also discovered something else. She saw that the serrated knife Maggie-Lynn had buried into the duffel bag ended up sticking itself right through Tildra's black binder. Curious, Charm picked up the binder too.

Billy watched as Charm absently pocketed the scissors and focused her attention on removing the serrated knife from the binder, twisting it until she could dislodge it and pull it out. She dropped the knife back into the duffel bag. Then she stood and opened the binder.

Charm laid her eyes upon *LAZY DOODLE #399*—the sketch of Billy tortured. She stared at it a moment before tearing it out and letting it go, where it slowly glided back and forth in the air while falling to the floor.

That's when Charm beheld *LAZY DOODLE #398*. A very well-drawn sketch of herself, Charm Wilson, freckles and all, lying on the floor with stab wounds in her stomach and face. Charm glanced down and saw that Tildra's corpse appeared coincidentally similar to how Charm's body was depicted in the sketch. Charm had stabbed Tildra in real life right where Tildra had stabbed Charm on paper.

Charm threw her head back and roared with laughter. Then she lazily tossed the binder down onto Tildra's corpse, where it landed directly on her dead face, covering it.

She turned to the boy and pulled the scissors from her pocket. "I ain't gonna hurt you in any way, Billy. It's over. I'm gonna cut you free. Just needed these handy scissors first. I'm sorry for the delay. I'm just . . . not thinking straight. Gonna cut you free right now."

Charm walked over and stood before him. "After which, would it be okay if we had a conversation?" She swallowed hard.

Billy looked up at her, his face pale, his cheek bruised red, purple tape across his mouth. He nodded.

* * *

Instead of coming forward to free him, Billy watched Charm suddenly turn and dart back to the duffel bag, reaching down into it with both hands and pulling out one of the small black pillows.

And the serrated knife.

Billy leaned back into the brick wall, tensing up out of instinct and anxiety.

"It's for you to hold," Charm said quickly, holding the

knife up with two fingers, the blade facing the floor. "I'm gonna set it down next to you. So you can feel safe while we talk."

She walked back over, placing the little pillow down in front of her and kneeling on it. She slid the knife across the floor to Billy's side. It scraped along the dirty bricks, coming to a rest beside his right knee. Charm reached forward and grabbed a tip of the purple duct tape across his mouth.

"Might sting," she said. "I'm gonna rip it off all at once."

He jerked his head yes, grateful but impatient. Charm ripped the tape off.

Billy moved his lips around, then opened and closed his jaw a few times. A single tear of overwhelming relief ran down his cheek. "Nah, that wasn't too bad," he mumbled. "Best feeling I've had all night, actually."

Charm cut through the tape around his lower half. Billy stretched out his legs. Slowly though because they were numb and tingling. Next, Charm leaned up and carefully cut through the tape around his wrists above his head. As she cut away, her eyes focused on her task, Billy gave her a stare. He didn't know what to make of her.

Then he gave an immense sigh as his arms fell to his sides.

"Oh, that's wonderful," he said in a loud whisper. He caressed his wrists, holding his hands in his lap, letting them relax. Then he remembered the knife beside him and quickly seized it into grasp, gripping it as tightly as he could —which wasn't tight at all. He could barely hold it.

Charm leaned back and just knelt there, covered in blood, fiddling with the red scissors, her busted lip growing more swollen and purple by the minute.

They were silent awhile.

Billy released another heavy sigh. The ordeal was seemingly over. He was ever thankful to be alive but also now found himself suddenly feeling irritated, able to focus more on the injustice done to him now that he was free.

"Thanks," he said. "I guess."

Charm said nothing. She did notice him eyeing the scissors she was twiddling between her thumbs, so she tossed them through the air and across the room, where they landed in the center of the open duffel bag.

Billy looked past Charm's shoulder at Tildra's body, a bony bundle of bloodied black sheet-robe, black binder laying open over her head.

"I can't believe she was secretly evil this whole time," he said. "I had the biggest crush ever on her."

Once more Charm said nothing.

"Did she ever like me?" Billy asked.

Charm took a deep breath and gently blew the air out, puffing her lips. "I've never seen anyone more excited about something than her about killing you. But yeah, she did say she liked you in the beginning."

"So why did she wanna kill me?"

"Uhhh." Charm scratched the outside of one of her nostrils with a forefinger, thinking. "I don't know," she said at last. "I only met her tonight, Billy. I've been in the city with my cousins all summer."

Billy was dumbfounded, confused at that. "Then what the hell are you even doing here? How did this all happen?"

"I thought this was all a prank!" she squeaked, her voice panicky all of a sudden. "I'm really stupid and really sorry."

"*What*?" Billy said, incredulous.

"Look," Charm started. "I overheard them when I was goin' pee! Only just a bit ago. They were gonna kill us both!"

Billy scoffed. "Oh, well, never mind that they were gonna kill me the whole time."

Charm was flustered. "Again, Billy—" She held up her hands in defense. "I thought this was all just a prank—"

"How's that?" Billy snapped.

"I didn't know they were gonna kill you for real until twenty minutes ago!"

He was taken aback, and she seized the moment. "I know it was really, really mean, but I thought this was just all a nasty prank to scare you into leaving Tildra alone. Until I overheard them while I was goin' pee! Talking about how real it actually was—that they were gonna kill you and kill me too!"

Billy stared at her, considering. He nodded—for a good few seconds—before saying, "You're a liar, Charm."

"Beg pardon?" Her tone was one of great offense.

"Why would you take off your mask earlier if it was just gonna be a prank, knowing full well I could easily tell on you later? Why would *you* hit me on the *head* if it was just a prank? A pumpkin? Really!?"

Charm stared at him. Her lips moved to form words, but no words came out. Then she closed her eyes and sighed. "Darn it."

Billy scoffed again, spittle flying from his mouth this time. "Seriously?!"

"I made sure you didn't see me." Charm's eyes were still closed. "I was hoping you might think it was Tildra or Magg, what with the light shining in your face."

"Just say what you wanted to talk about, Charm."

Charm swallowed, pale, looking at him again. "You're right. I'm such a fool to lie. Look, Billy. I'm scared of getting into trouble."

"I bet you are," he acknowledged.

"Listen," Charm said sternly. She hunched her shoulders, her eyebrows shaped like a wide V. She meant business now. "Okay, I knew they were gonna kill you the whole time. But I wasn't ever gonna let them. I just had to play along at first."

Billy rolled his eyes.

"I mean it!" she shouted. "It wasn't an option to stay behind and call the police. What if the girls decided to call it off for some reason, or what if you didn't show up? That would've just been *wildly* awkward, you know what I'm saying?"

"Wouldn't have bothered me," Billy said, straight-faced.

Charm's confidence at that moment wouldn't be budged, though. Billy could see the resolve reflected in her eyes as she laid out her case before him. "Okay, but what if they woulda killed you before the cops even got here? Think about it, dummy. I had to say yes to them because I had to come with them, to see what would happen—try to stop it if I could. I couldn't try talking them out of it because it would've made them suspicious of me, and I might not have been able to help you. So I did play along. I laughed and joked and pretended to be evil with them. I took part in the ritual. And yeah, I knocked you out with a pumpkin. Which, quite frankly, you should be thanking me for, Billy Tippard. Magg wanted to give you a concussion with a big ass branch, but instead I volunteered to do it and used the squishiest pumpkin I could find. I was looking out for you."

Billy took her words in, blinking in surprise as her story settled into his mind, forming up with his memories and providing a dash of clarity to the mystery surrounding the night's events. So far, he couldn't say her words didn't fit.

Charm jerked a thumb over her shoulder. "I saw the drawing Tildra did of you being tortured. I'm so sorry you had to go through that, her showing it to you. I just saw that she drew one of me too."

Billy could feel his eyes stretching wide with realization. He certainly remembered the drawings. That first one Tildra showed him—the one Tildra had said was a secret glimpse of the future—it *was* of Charm. He knew that clearly now. They really were going to kill her too.

Charm continued. "I couldn't help you at first because I was unarmed and afraid they'd overpower me if I tried anything. I had to be strategic, wait for my time. And then they gave me that pocketknife! Which, to be honest, I don't know why they did that. Thrill of there being some risk to it, maybe? I don't know. Either way, they're together in the netherworld now, regretting that mistake."

Billy didn't know what to think.

"I killed them before they killed us," Charm said, wiping her eyes before they could release tears. "That's what happened. No lies. I'm sorry you had to go through all this, but I was never gonna let it go all the way. And if you really look at tonight, I'm sure you can see I've been protecting you this whole time."

Billy couldn't make sense of anything anymore. His mind had turned to mush. All he really knew for sure was that, well, he was indeed alive because of Charm.

"So then . . ." He spoke groggily, as if rising from a dream. He picked his ear, then flicked whatever was in it off his finger while mulling over Charm's story. Finally, "So then, shoot! Why didn't you just say all that right from the get-go?"

Charm looked like the answer was obvious. "Didn't think you'd buy it."

"But you thought I'd buy the prank story?"

She shrugged. "Sometimes the truth is hardest to believe. Sometimes . . . the truth is just that absurd."

Billy stewed on that for a moment. He loosened his

already questionable grip on the serrated knife, holding it absently now. "I get that. I do. Especially when you can still go down for assaulting me with a pumpkin. Also, you did kind of attack them first. Your situation's complicated."

"Billy, please. All you need to do is say you don't remember anything other than—"

"You really did kill the hell outta them both," he interrupted, glancing between the two corpses.

"And I don't regret it," Charm said. "I'm sure it's gonna mess me up inside for years, and I'll probably need therapy and all that, but it was the right thing to—"

"So they were gonna start a serial killing secret society and do me in first?" he asked.

"They were actually gonna do *me* in first—but yes." She wiped her eyes again, ignoring the splotches of blood over the rest of her face. She sniffed. "I did think it was incredibly stupid and wrong. I'll admit I enjoy reading about all that kind of stuff. Murder and mayhem is fascinating—in books and TV. But in real life? *No.* Stopping it from happening was the only thing that mattered tonight, and—"

"Okay, Charm, enough," Billy insisted. He was almost annoyed. "I know you saved our lives. I'll return the favor however I can. I am grateful."

Charm gave a sudden sob of relief, overwhelmed. "Thank you. Thank you, Billy."

Billy found himself unable to take his eyes off Tildra's lifeless body. "That monster manipulated me. Turned your best friend against us too."

"To be fair," Charm risked saying, "I think Magg was already against you."

There was a brief moment of silence before the two actually shared a slight chuckle. Then those chuckles turned into a shared laugh.

"Yeah," he admitted with a tired smile. "I've always felt she was just fake-nice to me. If that."

"I know why," Charm revealed. "Or part of why, at least. My ninth birthday party, Billy. Right when she came into the kitchen to get a piece of cake, you turned around and sneezed on her."

"What? I don't remember that!"

"I didn't see it. But yeah, right on her, she said." Charm carried on a laugh she seemingly couldn't stifle, even though she was alone in her humor now. "Said you made her spill her drink over her dress too. And that it all happened in front of the few cool kids that actually came that day. She was so red." Another giggle. "*That* I remember. I always thought that story was funny."

"Well, that's all it was. A story." His tone was intentionally stubborn, indicating that'd be the end of it. "You think we could get outta here now, Charm? Pretty sure I'm scarred for life."

4

———

When they first arrived, the girls had hidden their bikes between two hedges about halfway up the hill. Now, Billy sat on Charm's handlebars. She rode them down the stone path toward the cemetery entrance, where Billy's own bike rested behind a bush along an old, dilapidated wooden gate.

Billy hopped off, grabbed his bike, got on it, then pulled around and parked his front wheel right before Charm's, where they faced one another. The stars shined bright above them, casting a pale glow on the night, almost like a see-through mist.

Charm could see something was nagging at Billy.

"Listen," he began. "I'm just gonna ask once, and then I'll never ask again, Charm, I promise. I know you saved my life, but were you ever gonna not save my life? Before you overheard them planning to betray you, were you gonna join their secret society? It's okay—either way, you saved me in the end. I just wanna know."

Charm, covered in blood with her big, busted lip, just wanted to go home. She gave him a look of plain emptiness.

"I shouldn't have hit you with the pumpkin," she said,

slow and calm, as if testifying before the court. "I should've been smart enough to find another way. I wasn't, and I'm sorry for that. But like you said, you know I saved your life, Billy. Don't know how else to prove it. So, you have to understand, you asking me something like that—it makes me feel like *my* life is on the line. So I don't mean to be mean, but if you try and get me in trouble, I'll lash out. I'll tell the whole school the truth—that Tildra wanted to kill you 'cause she saw you eat your own booger."

It may have been a weak threat in the grand scheme of things, but Charm strongly suspected it would work on Billy, who she knew was always wary of being embarrassed, being made fun of. His face lost all color except for the red bruise on his cheek, and he staggered back a step, the two wheels of his bike rolling with him—exactly the reaction Charm had hoped for.

"What?" he croaked. "I've never done that."

"Besides, nobody would believe you if you told on me," Charm continued matter-of-factly. "The reality is, I stopped you from dying tonight. You're here right now. Alive. I could just as easily have killed you too and blamed it on Magg and Tildra. *And* you forget I gave you the knife when I cut you free, to help you feel safe. I was scared you might run off before we talked, scared you might even try to stab me, but I still cut you free—because it was the right thing to do. So no, I never considered killing you, Billy. But I think you might already know that by now. To be honest, I think we're both just shaken up and acting weird. Thinking weird. You know?"

Billy gazed at her. Charm noticed he had a little sliver of pumpkin gut wrapped around a seed stuck in his hair.

"I . . ." He trailed off, then cleared his throat and swallowed. "Yeah. Okay. I'm sorry. It's just this whole night, I mean. Scariest night of my life. I'm sorry, Charm."

"Hey, we got through it," she said. "We showed those girls who's boss. And you stood up to all of us! Or did your best to, at least. Be proud. Now, come on. Let's go home, tell our parents what happened, and try to recover."

"Sounds like a plan," he muttered.

They each turned their bikes around, Charm confident and with purpose, Billy absent-minded as if stuck in a trance, and rode off in opposite directions.

Charm shouted back, "Call the cops when you get home. But wait like thirty minutes! Give me time to call first! Night, Billy!"

"Yes, ma'am," Billy replied, using a regular indoor voice, unaware just how traumatized he actually was. "See you, Charm. Thank you."

5

JUST BEFORE THE SECOND NIGHT

Billy was zoned out in his family sitting room, thinking about the night before. He realized where he was again and glanced up at Detective Dave, who was looking at him. It was clear by the detective's expression that he had asked Billy something and was waiting for a reply.

"No worries," Detective Dave said, jotting a quick note in his portfolio. "We'll get the whole story from Charm, then." What Dave said next sounded more like a thought to himself, stated aloud. "I'll be damned, so she killed her own friends to stop them from killing you. Girl's a hero."

Billy couldn't help feeling his face scrunch up sourly after the last sentence.

Detective Dave noticed. "Hey. Listen, son," he said, softening his gravelly tone. He leaned forward in his seat. "What you went through took a lotta courage as well—"

"You know, I think it might o' been Charm who hit me in the head with that pumpkin," Billy decided to say.

Dave cocked his head. "You mean the other one? Tildra? You said Charm."

"I . . . I meant Charm."

Dave looked confused. "Why would she assault you, then save your life?"

Billy had to admit it was a fair question.

"Did you see Charm hit you with your own eyes?" Detective Dave asked.

"I didn't. It's just . . ."

"Well, you said yourself you couldn't see. Them girls were shining a light in your face, that right?"

"Yes, but—"

"So maybe the girl you liked hit you. If you think about it, that's a lot more likely."

"Charm hit me in the head with that pumpkin."

Dave furrowed his brows. "Where's this coming from? You just said you didn't see her when you got hit."

"Maybe she was hiding."

"Well, we'll get the details from her, believe you me. She thought she was playing a prank, you said. Now that is mean, I'll grant you. I could understand if you're sore at her. But again, you didn't see her hit you—though you did see her save your life."

"I just feel anxious about it all. Something's off about how everything happened. I know it."

"Okay, look. You told me everything you know, right?"

Billy assured Charm he would tell the cops only that he got knocked out and woke up to her saving his life—and until now that was pretty much all he had said, both to his mother and to Detective Dave. He understood why Charm wanted the rest kept private. Her assaulting him with a pumpkin, playing along with the murder plan, and preemptively killing two other girls all so she could make sure he, in fact, wouldn't be murdered—well, that just wasn't the best story to tell the police, even if it was true. And while Billy did have some lingering suspicions about her intentions, he still mostly wanted to protect Charm for saving him. It was only the detective calling her a *hero* in front of him that made him realize how conflicted he was and spurred him to reveal that she was the pumpkin-smasher. But he had said enough. Billy honestly didn't know if he believed Charm's story or not, and as much as he might've wanted to tell on her for everything just in case, he also knew he didn't want to harm her if she really had planned to save him the whole time. After all, at the end of the night, he was alive because of her actions.

So, begrudgingly, he gave her the benefit of the doubt. "Yes. I told you everything."

"Okay, then," Detective Dave said. "See, I think you not knowing exactly how you got hit in the head is making you jump to wild thoughts. But it just doesn't make sense that she would hurt you, then help you. And regardless, she saved your life. Whatever happened before, with her gunning to prank you, sometimes it's better to let bygones be just that. This is a small town, it's important to stay on good terms with people. Let things go, second chances, however you wanna look at it. It's part o' growing up."

"But you'll find the pumpkin though, right?" Billy suddenly had the urge to ask. "See whose fingerprints are on it? It's all smashed, but I know it's at the top of the big hill. Shouldn't be too hard to find the big pieces."

Detective Dave sighed. Then he smiled. "Sure, fine, you're darn tootin'. And I'll tell you what, we're gonna get the full story from Charm. Figure out just how all this came to pass. But no matter what happens, this is still a happy ending for Billy Tippard. You just remember that, okay?"

6

JUST BEFORE THE SECOND NIGHT

Officer Sherry Merwittle stared at the corpse of the kid named Maggie-Lynn McMillan, who was face-down in a rusty old toilet, covered in dried blood with several flies buzzing around her.

Sherry was kneeling in the doorway of the stall, studying the body while puffing on a cigarette.

A male voice shouted from outside the restroom. "Hey, Sherry!"

Exhaling a cloud, Sherry panicked, fanning away the smoke and dropping the cigarette into the toilet between the dead girl's head and the brim of the seat. She'd needed the nicotine fix after entering the restroom and laying eyes on the bloodbath, but she also didn't want anyone seeing her smoke around a crime scene. Not that it really mattered or that anyone would care—Sherry suspected there wouldn't be much of an on-site investigation. The fellas would snap a few dozen photographs, of which maybe a handful would come out okay. The rest would be out of focus. Additionally, half-assed notes detailing what the scene was like would be taken and then placed in a file cabinet. And that would be the end of it. The chief would say to clean it up. It wasn't like anything in their little town would ever become high-profile anyway.

So perhaps not in spite of all the incompetence but rather because of it, Sherry took a small pride in maintaining a sense—or at least the charade—of professional decorum on her part.

"Yeah, Ryan, what's up!?" she shouted back at her colleague. Officer Ryan was the precinct slacker who usually sat by the phone all day playing solitaire and watching sitcom reruns. He didn't even bother to enter the restroom, electing to shout from the outside instead.

"Got Dave out here on the radio! Wants to know if you want the lead on this! Be a hell of a first case, Detective—so long as you don't accidentally throw your fist up the horse's ass!"

Sherry was stunned. She'd taken the written exam last month and only just been made detective this week. "This whole deal? Mine? I get to solve this!?"

"It's already solved, stupid! I'll take that as a yes. Dave said to go to the Wilson girl's house. He'll meet you there. Hear the girl's side o' things."

Sherry stood and turned, making her way out of the restroom. "Oh, hell yes, I want it!" she answered. "Okay, I'm—"

In her haste, Sherry tripped over Tildra's corpse, accidentally kicking the black binder off the dead kid's head.

"Oh, shoot."

Tildra's eyes were wide open, staring at the ceiling. Sherry picked up the binder and delicately placed it back on top of her blood-crusted face, just how it was.

Sherry remained kneeling there for a moment, wondering.

"Fist up a horse's ass?" she muttered to herself. "The hell does that even mean? *Dumbass Ryan.*"

Sherry stood and walked out of the restroom, leaving behind the two dead children with flies buzzing over them. The thick old tree covered in a century's worth of carvings loomed just visible outside the propped-open doorway, with sunlight flooding in as much as it could, those golden rays shining in through the bare window on the far wall as well.

JUST BEFORE THE STORM

1

THE SECOND NIGHT

Officer Sherry gave Charm the major stink-eye, squinting at her, nostrils flared. Sherry sensed it—the horseshit wafting directly from Charm's aura—now able to see right through the girl. It was because of something the kid had said earlier, something that just didn't fit. She didn't know how much Charm was lying and hiding, but she knew the kid was lying and hiding something—and Sherry meant to discover the whole of it.

The rest of the kitchen was of course oblivious to Sherry's racing mind as Charm told the climax of her story, no longer able to keep the tears at bay, which now fell freely. "I strangled her," she managed to mumble through the waterworks. "I didn't have to do that."

"Listen, child," Julia said. "You don't ever dare beat yourself up over that. I'm forever thankful you did it."

"That's right," Ralph topped off.

From her corner by the fridge, Betts scanned the room as she was used to doing and noticed Officer Sherry giving Charm the stink-eye. So Betts, surprised, gave Sherry the stink-eye. Sherry never noticed.

Detective Dave agreed with Julia and Ralph. "All things considered, everything you did is understandable, Charm. You were fighting for your life. We get it."

Sherry looked Charm over, studying the girl's eyes, her expressions, patiently waiting for just the right moment to pry for information.

Meanwhile, out the kitchen window over the sink, a shadowed figure in the starlit night could be seen riding up on their bike from down the gravel road—unkempt, messy hair thrown about with each pedal.

"And you need to understand that too," Dave was hammering home to Charm. "You have no shame to bear in any of this. They were trying to stab you and you fought back. It was self-defense, all of it. No doubt about it."

Charm sniffled. "Well, anyhow," she said, ignoring the praise. "I cut Billy free after, told him what I could about everything. Then we left."

Betts raised her chin and squinted out the window. "I believe young William is here."

Officer Sherry looked out the window and saw a boy in the front yard, hopping off his bike, dropping it on the grass.

"Oh, good!" Julia declared to the room, pleased. She looked at Betts. "And it's just Billy. Not William."

"What?" Charm said, sitting up straight. "Billy's here?"

Betts turned to Julia, looking almost aghast, a hand covering her mouth. "But Billy is supposed to be a *nickname* for William. And William is a *saint's* name. William of Perth is one of Christ's *saints*."

"Uh-huh," Julia answered Charm. "I wanted him to come thank you in front of everybody. Formally, I guess. It'd mean a lot to me." She looked back at Betts. "And I'm sure he was one of the good saints. But I don't *like* the name William."

"I'm just yankin' your chain, darlin'." Betts smirked, lazily waving away any offenses given or taken. "Just a joke." And before Julia could respond, Betts turned and took three long strides, making her way to the front door to let Billy in.

But then Sherry casually stepped in front of Betts and went toward the door herself. "It's okay. I got it."

Officer Sherry hadn't known Billy would be coming and was cautiously excited by the development. She hadn't met the boy and was very much curious about him. The front door was one step to the left out of the kitchen, and she opened it just as Billy reached the porch.

He stood there, waved hello. Sherry offered him her hand. "Good evening! I'm happy you're safe, Billy. I'm Officer Sherry."

"Hi." They shook hands.

"Well, actually," Sherry said, still shaking his limp arm, "I just made detective. And you're my first case. So, I guess it'd be *Detective* Sherry, now."

Back in the kitchen, Detective Dave heard this comment from the table and rolled his eyes. Ralph saw and uttered a low laugh.

Billy walked into the kitchen, Officer Sherry behind him. Everyone looked at him, taking in his gaunt appearance and bright red cheek.

Billy waved. "Hey, y'all."

Detective Dave, Ralph, and Betts greeted him with a kind nod in unison. Charm just stared.

"Hey, baby," Julia said. "Come here."

Billy went beside his mother at the table.

"How are you, kid?" Ralph asked him with a soft punch on the shoulder.

"Good," Billy answered.

"Good," Ralph said.

Julia put her arm around her son and turned him toward Charm. "Okay, if y'all don't mind," she said to everyone, "Billy has something he'd like to say."

"Sure," Dave said, closing his portfolio. "We can just about finish up afterwards."

Julia quickly tugged Billy's arm and whispered something in his ear. He stood back up straight. "I want you to know that if last night would've ended up just being the prank you thought it was, I forgive you," he told Charm. "I don't want you to feel bad about anything or have any guilt."

It sounded rehearsed. Everyone could tell, his voice monotone. But they just assumed he was performing the customary courtesies his mother prescribed for having his life saved. Nobody thought anything of it.

Except Officer Sherry. She studied Billy now. He was empty-eyed like a zombie, reciting lines without a thought simply to ease his mother's heart, while Charm sat there looking almost pleased, albeit straight-faced, still a tad teary-eyed.

Billy continued. "And I want to thank you again for saving my—"

"If I could butt in for just a jiff," Sherry said.

Everyone in the little kitchen jerked their heads to her at once, all in disbelief. Even Billy was stunned.

"Thank you," Sherry said in response. "There is something, just real quick, that needs to be accounted for."

"Excuse me?" Julia almost shouted, not trying to hide her irritation in the slightest. "Why would you interrupt?"

"Because she's a clueless weirdo," Ralph answered under his breath.

"Sherry," Detective Dave said in a low tone, gentle but firm. "Sherry, whatever it is, it can wait a moment."

Officer Sherry ignored them all and kept her eyes locked

on Billy, saying, "All you remember is getting hit on the head at the cemetery and then waking up inside the restroom, restrained. That's correct?"

"Umm, yes, ma'am," Billy said.

Sherry regarded him. "I was in that restroom today. There's nothing in there that could've been used to hit you on top of the head and knock you out."

That's when Charm joined the proceedings. "Wasn't it . . ." She trailed off a moment, forehead scrunched, thinking. Then she looked at Billy. "A pumpkin you said, right?"

Billy stared at her. "Right." He kept his unblinking look on her. "I had the guts and seeds all over me. Remember?"

"I do," Charm said, wide-eyed, as though suddenly recalling. "Of course. Sorry."

The other adults in the kitchen had gone from perplexed that Officer Sherry had interrupted to now visibly annoyed. Detective Dave leaned to his left. "I apologize," he muttered to Julia.

"That's what I was told too," Sherry said. "A pumpkin. Thing is, there wasn't any pumpkin in that bathroom."

Charm looked puzzled. "Didn't Billy just confirm to you that he got hit outside?"

Ralph couldn't help but chuckle.

"Yes, he did," Sherry said, answering Charm. "But *you* said Tildra and Billy walked in the restroom together while you and Maggie-Lynn waited outside. *You* said Tildra was gonna take his clothes—that that was the prank."

Billy, surprised at that, blushed hard, making both of his cheeks red.

"Oh," Charm uttered. "Well, that's what they told me the prank was."

"So Billy got knocked out with a pumpkin, then just

casually stood up and strolled into the restroom with Tildra?" Officer Sherry asked.

"I don't know how that part happened," Charm said. "I wasn't present when it took place."

Again, Billy stared at Charm.

Officer Sherry frowned. "You were waiting outside the restroom but didn't see them going *in* the restroom?"

"I was *using* the restroom at the time—the boys' side. Tildra said to use the boys' side if we had to go. I came back out and Magg was there. She said Tildra and Billy had gone into the girls' side. We waited until Tildra came back out and asked if we wanted to come in and see."

Sherry was out of questions. She bit her lip, desperately trying to think of another hole in the girl's story, but Charm's tracks were well-covered.

"Well—" Sherry tried weakly.

"This could've waited, Detective," Dave said. "There's always going to be loose ends, easily gathered in due time. What's fact is she saved this boy's life, and we're here to honor that. We're here to support this girl."

Over in her corner, Betts held just the hint of a smile, proud of her grand-goddaughter for sticking up for herself against—from Betts's perspective—such an incompetent, overzealous, damnfool detective.

Officer Sherry could only nod and acknowledge defeat. "Right. Well . . . just following my investigative instinct."

Julia shook her head in disbelief.

"Sure. Honed and perfected after only a day," Ralph said, unable to stifle the sarcasm.

"I do think it was a fair line of inquiry," Sherry said, shooting him a look. "But Dave's right. I could've asked later." She looked around at everyone. "I'm sorry. I still need work on listening to my head over my gut." She gestured to

Billy with a low hand. "By all means, finish your 'Thank You' from earlier."

Now, at this point in the evening, Officer Sherry's behavior—her derailing interruptions and awkward etiquette—surprised nobody. But the room stared at her regardless, in awe. They were collectively amazed at how she could be so unaware of being so genuinely embarrassing—and it made them all feel pity for her, even though they still thought her unbearable.

Billy seemed unable to respond. He glanced back and forth between Charm and Officer Sherry, taking in measured breaths as if trying to fight the nerves and work himself up to say something, looking unsettled and indecisive.

Meanwhile, Ralph turned in his seat, politely covered his own mouth and released a single, sharp cough.

Billy shut his eyes and squealed, "It was Charm who hit me with a pumpkin!"

2

———

It took the room a second to realize it was stunned. Everyone's expression was confused—as if they either didn't understand what Billy had said or were waiting for him to say he misspoke.

"Huh?" Charm let out, most surprised of all. Her eyes took on a wary, threatened gaze.

She looked scared.

"Tildra, you mean." Julia touched her son's elbow. "Right, sweetie? You said Charm."

"Yes," Billy nodded. "Charm." He pointed right at her, finger nearly in her face, perhaps a bit more confident now that he'd already said it. "Charm smashed the pumpkin on my head."

Several gasps rang out.

Officer Sherry's jaw dropped.

Even the ordinarily stone face of Betts was shocked. Betts had been standing in her corner, arms crossed and leaning against the fridge, looking regal and relaxed most of the night. Now—still standing in that same position—she appeared stiff and anxious, her expression dismayed.

Ralph, however, had no further time to waste on being surprised. He turned in his chair toward Billy, his face almost level with the boy's, glaring right at him. "Come again?"

Billy ignored him. Instead, he addressed the rest of the kitchen but kept his gaze on Charm. "They had me taped up against a wall, and then Maggie-Lynn, Tildra, and *Charm* all took part in some demonic ritual thing with the masks and robes and stuff and told me they were gonna kill me."

Julia, utterly flabbergasted, abruptly leaned back in her chair as though shoved by a wind, the features of her face thrown back and sunken in. She moved her lips to speak but was unable to form speech.

Sherry jerked her head at Dave. "I thought you said you interviewed this kid?"

Detective Dave held up a finger with his mouth open. No words came out.

Charm's voice broke the silence. She gazed at Billy with water in her eyes. "I'm . . . I'm really sorry. If I was you, I wouldn't think I was any type of hero either. I don't—I don't blame you if you hate me." A single tear ran down her right cheek, followed by a long blink of the eyes and two more teardrops racing down her left. "But it ain't fair for you to lie. *Please*, Billy."

Billy turned to Officer Sherry. "I did tell Mr. Dave earlier today. But he didn't believe me."

"Now hold on!" Dave said, agitated all of a sudden. "Don't twist it up. He didn't see anyone hit him on the head. Those girls were shining a light in his face—a flashlight. He didn't see shit. I told him he was confused. I mean, Charm saved his life for God's sake! That's what we know. And, according to Billy this entire time, that's *all* he knows."

"Damn right," Ralph said. He gave Detective Dave a nod

of gratitude before turning back to Billy. "It's fine, kid. You went through something really harrowing. Who are we to judge?"

Billy ignored them, staring Charm down and willing himself to voice his truest gut instinct. "You might be a good person now, but I don't think you were when this began—and I want *that* Charm to answer for herself."

Betts uncrossed her arms and took a step forward. Nobody noticed.

Charm's breathing became loud. She shook her head at Billy, denying his assessment.

"You didn't tell me any of this," Julia said to her son, still looking confused.

"I wasn't sure if I was gonna come out with it," Billy admitted. "I was conflicted."

"Enough," Ralph scolded, though it sounded like he was pleading.

"Mrs. Tippard," Detective Dave said. "It might be best if you and Billy head on home for the evening."

But Billy would not be silenced. "I believed her! She won! She had me!" He turned back to Charm. "But, you know what? I remembered something. Something you said to Maggie-Lynn right after you gutted Tildra. You told her you changed your mind. That you decided you wanted to be a hero instead. Why would you say that if you were gonna be the hero all along? Why not tell Maggie-Lynn how you were gonna save me the whole time? I think it's because you were gonna kill me the whole time. Up until you found out they were gonna kill you too, which wasn't 'til the last minute I bet—"

"Not true!" Charm yelled. "I only told it to her like that 'cause I was mad at her, Billy! Honest!"

"—So *screw you*, Charm Wilson!" Billy yelled back. "I

changed my mind too. I'm telling everything!" He suddenly laughed hard, almost manically. "And guess what else? I'm thinking I'll have my momma buy me a hamster. Shoot, I might even get *three*! *Three* hamsters to start my *own* collection!" He delivered the last few lines viciously, in as sharp a tone as he could, a secret middle-finger just for Charm.

However, Billy didn't foresee just how bizarre of a thing that was to say, and Charm feigned complete ignorance, raising an eyebrow. There was a moment of silence.

"Well, obviously the boy's been through a lot," Ralph said. Then, under his breath, "Possibly concussed."

"Billy, baby," Julia said sweetly, touching his arm again. "It's like the detective said. You didn't see who hit you. Perhaps—perhaps knowing the other two girls are gone makes you want to hold Charm accountable for something?"

Billy, in disbelief, couldn't respond. He huffed and shook his head, frustrated.

"Maybe we should call this a night," Ralph said. He glanced around at Officer Sherry, Julia, Billy. "There's no hard feelings, of course."

Julia and Detective Dave seemed to think the suggestion reasonable. Dave was nodding, and Julia actually picked up her purse from beside her chair, gently slinging it over her shoulder. Even Billy was looking at the floor, quiet now that he'd said his piece and the burden was off his chest.

But Officer Sherry knew she couldn't relent, not if the truth was to have a chance.

"I'm sorry, but this is my investigation," she reminded everyone. "And I gotta do what's best for the case. I think we're gonna have to arrest Charm for questioning—"

"Over my dead body!" Ralph roared from his seat,

astounded, while horror struck Charm's face next to him, her eyes and mouth wide with a shaking fright.

"Sherry," Detective Dave croaked, his face skull-white. "We'll do no such thing."

"Detain!" Officer Sherry corrected herself, forcing a laugh and waving her arms to try and calm the confined room. "I am so sorry! I meant detain! I didn't mean arrest. I meant she's gonna be *detained* for questioning."

"Let me tell you something, Sherry," Dave said, looking up at her with suddenly straight posture from the table. "I'm in charge here and I will say what happens. And tonight, we are here in the capacity of supporting this girl."

"Okay," Julia said. "Maybe I actually wouldn't mind the questioning."

Ralph scoffed. "Are you serious?"

"Just the questioning part!" she defended. "To help get the full story. My boy can be questioned more too."

Trembling all over, Charm said, "Everything I did, I did to save Billy."

"Then you have nothing to hide, sweetheart," Julia told her.

Ralph leaned forward at the table, staring up at Officer Sherry with every vein and muscle in his face tightened. "My daughter's a hero," he said with stone authority. "She's not leaving this house."

"Let's go, Charm," Sherry said.

"Dave!" Ralph pleaded in a high-pitched voice.

Detective Dave turned to Julia in his seat. "You and your boy should go home." He turned to Sherry. Beads of sweat had begun to form on his brow. "And I think you should go back to the graveyard and help monitor the crime scene. Right away, please."

"You put me on this case," Officer Sherry said. "It's mine

now. I appreciate you showing me the ropes, but if you have a complaint, take it to the chief. In the meantime, I'm detaining her for questioning. She's coming with me to the station and that's that."

Billy and Charm exchanged a look. Surprisingly, he seemed almost as scared as she was.

"I *made* you detective," Dave said in a low mumble under his breath, as if muffling the statement could make it inaudible to everyone but Sherry. "I *approved* you."

"And I appreciate it," Sherry said aloud. "I feel like I'm already making a difference." She looked at Charm. "Stand up."

Still looking at Billy, her breathing now ragged, Charm's face turned into a scowling grimace. She sprang up out of her chair and slapped her palms down onto the kitchen table. "Booger-eater!" she cried. "You can't prove any of your lies! I saved your life!"

Ralph agreed wholeheartedly. "You're goddamn right!"

"Don't yell at my son!" Julia said to both father and daughter. "He's been through a lot, like you said, Ralph. We all have!"

Billy shook his head, astonished. "You really are a bag of slime, Charm. I'm telling the truth and you know it."

"Prove it," she bellowed, standing before Billy with her arms planted like pillars on the little table—as if she were some sort of guardian statue, challenging him.

"I won't have to," he said. "Your fingerprints on the smashed pumpkin will."

Charm snorted. "No, they won't! I wore gloves last night, you idiot!"

The room was dead quiet again. Even Billy couldn't believe what he just heard. He stared at Charm with his mouth open.

Charm realized what she'd said and shook her head with a blushing laugh. "*Meaning* if I did do it, there wouldn't be prints because I wore gloves last night. Hellooo! Jeez, y'all. That came out wrong was all."

"You," Julia said softly, gazing at Charm with glossy eyes. "You were gonna kill my son?"

Charm shook her head violently, short sandy hair once more whipping wildly back and forth as her eyes welled up again. "Ma'am! No!"

Betts had spent the entirety of the evening studying the people in her kitchen. But now, for the first time, she couldn't help but lay her scrutinizing look on Charm.

"Are you kidding me!?" Ralph raved. "Your son is alive right now because of her!"

Detective Dave put a hand on Julia's forearm. "Take Billy home," he insisted.

A low wail escaped Charm's mouth as she looked down at the floor, shuddering.

"I'm not gonna cuff you, darlin'," Officer Sherry told her, as if that were somehow supposed to be comforting.

"I told you she's not leaving this house!" Ralph shouted. "Over my dead body!"

Without thinking about it, Sherry casually rested her right hand on her rather large sidearm. "Now, Mr. Wilson. I respect you very much—"

"How dare you put your hand on your weapon in my house!" Ralph exclaimed, his eyes nearly bursting out of their sockets. "My daughter is a hero!" Infuriated, he shot out of his chair, toppling it back to smack against the tile. He power-walked out of the kitchen in three steps and blasted the front door open with one hand, storming outside.

"Okay now," Betts said, fully emerging from her corner at last, standing at the table. "I've seen him like this only one other time—when Charm's mother died. It'll be very difficult for me to calm him down. I think it's best y'all leave, and we resume this when heads have cooled."

"I'm inclined to agree with her, Sherry," Detective Dave said.

Out the kitchen window over the sink—to no one's notice—Ralph could be seen walking into his shed adjacent the main house, the stars in the sky shining bright and glorious overhead. After a moment of shuffling around inside, he reemerged with a baseball bat. Ralph walked right back across the yard, skipped up the front porch, strode in through the front door and marched back into the kitchen, pointing the wooden bat at Officer Sherry with one arm.

"You have no authority to arrest my daughter!" he screamed. "You have no evidence! This boy is confused, so please leave my house right now!"

3

———

THIRTEEN YEARS BEFORE THE VIOLENT NIGHTS

7:39 P.M.

The rain smacked the house outside, and baby Charm wouldn't stop crying.

She was three days old and had so far slept most of the time—and slept peacefully. But the ceaseless roar of heavy rainfall was new and startling to her, so she was awake and shrieking while Betts sat at the tiny kitchen table, cradling her.

They'd all returned from the city hospital an hour earlier—while the sky was still clear—and within fifteen minutes their home had been destroyed on the inside. Ralph took a baseball bat to it while doing some shrieking of his own, performing a merging tune of shattered glass, fractured wood, and deep, guttural screams, all followed by the swift, pouring torrent outside. Ralph was the noise that actually woke up Charm. The sudden rain just kept her up. Only the kitchen was spared from Ralph's wrath while Betts and the baby were in it. And when Ralph was finished he entered the kitchen—young and broken and lathered in tears—and walked to the table, looking at the infant.

He leaned down and kissed Charm's forehead. Then he turned and headed back out of the room.

As a floorboard creaked under his receding steps, Betts thought now was as good a time as ever to redecorate the house and finally have tile put down in the kitchen. A new fridge too. Why not? More space for her magnets. She sat alone with the baby for a while. Thinking about life, thinking about nothing. Rain pelted the house from all sides, as if, Betts thought, their home was taking a long shower due to the nasty beating Ralph just gave it. But a shower wouldn't help, she knew. The rain couldn't wash away the wounds because all the wounds were on the inside. Only the love, glory, and power of our Almighty God could heal such internal wounds. Betts was also aware how erratic and peculiar these rushing thoughts were, and some deeper part of her understood she was undergoing the icy and numbing fog of grief.

The baby wailed.

Betts sat the three-day-old person on the edge of the small wooden table in front of her, with one hand supporting the baby's head, and leaned in, so that they were almost nose to nose.

"I'm the only one that all three of you have met," she said, and the baby fell silent, looking back at Betts, googly-eyed and curious. "Three generations now I've watched this family that will never know itself. You're the third of you. Your mother was the second. She's the one who died yesterday. She died because of complications from having you. Right before she died, she told me you were a good luck charm. She was happy to hold you . . . for the short moment that she did."

Betts stared at the baby. Charm's face shifted up and around continuously, reacting to the rain, following the sounds. The rain battered the house angrily, as if every bombarding drop was an exploding liquid rock. Charm cried out once more, and Betts cradled her again, slowly rocking her. The window over their kitchen sink was so blurry and wet that the outside world almost looked underwater. Charm's cries would not weaken or lessen, and Betts found herself thinking about all the ways to silence a child.

All the different ways.

After several more minutes, Betts sat the baby up on the table again, this time touching her nose to Charm's. The baby quieted. Betts smiled.

"The first of you was your grandmother. She was a bright, lively, but ultimately unhinged young bat who, on the night we met as kids, told me she had a secret she could never reveal, and that if her and I were going to be friends, I would have to respect that secret and never ask what it was. I never did. It might sound strange, but the fact that she would blatantly tell me she had a secret she couldn't reveal as opposed to just never mentioning it in the first place made me think of her as an open person I could trust. And she always was. Anyway, one night a few decades later—this was about a month after she gave birth to your mother—she decided to up and walk two miles down the dirt road to a neighboring farmstead and kill the entire family there with a sledgehammer while they was sleepin'. Then she walked back a mile to my old farm and knocked on my door. When I answered it, she was panting and covered in dust. Her hands and face were a pale purple. From exhaustion, I've always presumed—or exertion, rather. I asked her where her baby was, and she said not to worry, the baby was sleeping at home in her crib. I sat your grandmother down and poured her a glass of punch. She drank it down and told me what she did. Then she said she could reveal her long-kept secret. Your grandmother said her secret was that she was always meant to be a killer but had spent her life fighting the urge. She said she was descended from a family of killers, and that creatures—real, monstrous creatures—had visited her in dreams as a child and told those things directly to her. I didn't know how to react to any of that at first. I just stared at her. She stared back. What I did finally say was that I didn't believe her—even though I could feel she wasn't lying. I told her we were *all* descended from killers somehow or another, but that didn't mean we had to become killers ourselves. She laughed at that, saying it sounded pretty—but too late, 'cause her deed was done. She killed all four of them. Mother, father, son, daughter. For no other reason than to see if she could pull it off without anyone waking up. She succeeded, she said. Eventually, she stood up, saying she had to go—to visit new and worthy realms—and told me to come by her homestead the following day. It wasn't until then, as she left, that I noticed all the blood on her dark dress."

Charm drooled carelessly, her slobber dripping down onto the silk purple blanky she was swaddled in. Her wide little eyes were locked on Betts.

"Now, I had every intention of going to the law, but first I had to see it for myself. So when the sun rose, I walked to that neighboring farmstead and saw mother, father, son, and daughter all tucked under the covers with their brains bashed in. Then I walked to your grandmother's farm and found your mother in her crib, with the home otherwise abandoned. I took your mother with me and never saw your grandmother again. I reported her sins to both the authorities and the church. Then life went on. We moved into this house, and your mother became my daugh—"

Charm cried out louder than ever, right in Betts's face,

spritzing her nose and cheeks with baby drool. Rainfall soaked their window over the kitchen sink while their roof sang the sounds of breaking water.

"What happened to your mother yesterday is not your fault, child." Betts closed her eyes, shuddered, took a deep breath. "I very much want to kill you for it, but it's not your fault. I'm going to love you instead."

She cradled Charm again, produced a soft cloth, and began gently wiping around the baby's mouth.

4

THE SECOND NIGHT

9:37 P.M.

Without hesitation, Officer Sherry drew her service weapon and pointed it at Ralph.

"Please put the bat down," she said in a quick, calm voice.

Betts grabbed Charm with both arms and pulled her away from the table, back into the corner of the room. Julia followed suit and did the same with Billy, pulling him into the opposite corner of the kitchen, wrapping her arms around him and shielding him with her body.

"Put the gun down!" Charm shrieked. "Don't you point that at my daddy!"

"*I didn't mean for it to get like this!*" Billy shouted from his mother's arms with a voice now even higher-pitched than usual.

Detective Dave sat frozen in his chair, immobilized by shock.

Officer Sherry kept her gun on Ralph. She held a .44 Magnum, a considerable revolver. And Officer Sherry held it well—held it *still*. "Put the weapon down, sir," she said again in the calm, professional tone she'd practiced on end, over and over again in front of her bathroom mirror at home where she lived alone.

"My daughter ain't leaving!" Ralph yelled, tears rushing down his cheeks now.

"Your daughter will do whatever I lawfully command," Sherry declared. "I'm police."

"Put your gun down!" Charm pleaded. "Please, Detective Sherry!"

Only Detective Dave remained sitting at the table now, suddenly sweating profusely. Julia beckoned to him in a low voice from her corner behind him. "*Psst! Why aren't you doing anything?*"

The situation was no longer going smoothly for Detective Dave. He was overwhelmed, barely able to think, experiencing now what he had always worked so hard out of anxious fear to avoid: true conflict. But Dave didn't know how to articulate any of that, so instead he simply mumbled, "We . . . we've let this get out of hand, folks. Let's try to bring it down a notch. I prefer to keep things low stress."

"*What?*" Julia whispered, bewildered.

Ralph pointed at Charm with his free hand (bat-hand still on Sherry). "I'm putting my daughter in her bedroom, and then I'll be asking that you all politely leave! And then you can get in touch with *my attorney!*"

With her gun locked on Ralph, Officer Sherry remained resolute. "The girl's coming with me," she said in a stern, that's-the-end-of-it voice. "And you need to put the weapon down. *Right now.*"

From behind Detective Dave, Julia whispered to him again. "*You need to do something! Right now!*"

Ralph raised the bat above his head and screamed in his daughter's defense, the streaming tears almost jumping out of his eyes, lost in passionate rage. "You have no cause to detain her! If you take her to the station, the whole town will outcast her and judge her guilty! I'm not letting it happen! No way in hell!"

What happened next happened very fast.

Ralph took a step forward—toward Officer Sherry. Perhaps it was merely an instinctual step forward, meant to add emphasis to his words. Yet nonetheless, an aggressive step forward he took, bat raised above his head.

Sherry took serious aim at the center of mass.

"Now, by golly!" Detective Dave roared. Though trembling with anxiety, he overcame himself and rose to the task. He leaned forward and began to push himself up, putting his frame between Ralph and Sherry, shouting, "I will *not* let all hell break loose!"

When Officer Sherry pulled the trigger, it was Detective Dave's rising head between her and Ralph that exploded like a bursting red firework, splattering everyone else in the room with blood, all across their faces and clothes—understandable, being in such a cozy kitchen.

The bullet ricocheted off shattered skull and tore through one of the cupboard doors, lodging itself in the wall behind. Dave's practically headless corpse fell to its knees, then plopped down belly-first onto the floor with a heavy *THLUMP.*

It took about ten seconds for everyone to fully realize what had taken place. Not only because of how much more outrageous the situation became in that instant, but also because the gun blast was just so damn loud. They all flinched and grimaced at the sudden high-pitched gonging in their heads and quickly covered their ears.

All except Officer Sherry, who stood frozen as smoke slowly oozed out and rose from the muzzle of the gun she was still holding up with both hands. Her eyes were open, but it was as if she were unconscious. There were a few more long seconds of ear-ringing silence while the rest of the room went slack-jawed with astonishment.

"You shot him," Julia observed in a calm whisper. Then, "You fucking shot him! He's fucking dead!"

Strapped in his mother's arms in their corner of the tiny kitchen, Billy's face contorted into utter horror, his lower lip twitching. In Betts's arms in the opposite corner, Charm and her grand-godmother shared similar looks of shock, their wide-eyed faces splashed with drips of blood just like everyone else's.

Ralph lowered the bat, staring down at Detective Dave's dead body with a look of genuine sorrow. "Why'd you do that?" he asked Sherry. His tone was innocent and curious.

"It was an accident," Sherry answered, reclaiming awareness. Her voice was hoarse. "I meant to shoot you. You raised that bat at me—you took a step forward! It . . . it was a freak accident."

"You blew up his head!" Julia cried. "Fucking killed him!"

"I know, shut up!" Sherry couldn't find words. "I . . . He . . . His four daughters . . . It was an accident! He stepped in front of my gun—why would he do that!? You all saw it was an accident."

As Officer Sherry was speaking—almost frantically— and staring down at what was left of her colleague (the stump above Dave's neck leaked nonstop, spreading a slow blood-flood across the kitchen tile), Ralph quickly swung his bat down onto her right hand, smacking the gun from her grasp to the floor.

Sherry yelped and fell to her knees, debilitated by the sudden agony in her wrist, clutching it. Ralph stood over her, holding the bat above her head. "Move away from the gun!" he commanded. "I'm placing you under citizen's arrest for killing Dave!"

Sherry lunged for the gun.

Ralph smacked her hard on the back with the baseball bat. Sherry released a piercing scream but still managed to grab the gun and point it up at him from down on her knees.

"No." A weak whisper was all Charm could muster up.

As Ralph gripped the bat with both hands and brought it around to strike down again, Officer Sherry shot him twice in quick succession—once in the gut, once in the chest.

Everyone flinched and grimaced again during the two thunderous *BANGS!* that seemed to reverberate off the walls and vibrate the room. Ralph Wilson flew through the air with two red craters in his torso and crashed down onto the kitchen counter. The bat that was somehow still in his grasp smacked against the fridge and knocked a score of magnets to the floor—the framed picture of Charm and several of the crystal star magnets among them. Ralph's other arm flung around and knocked a wooden knife block off the counter, unleashing a dozen blades of different lengths to bounce and slip and slide across the bloody tile.

Then Ralph also hit the floor, face-down and dead, blood gushing from his mouth and gunshot wounds and quickly pooling around his body, where it would momentarily join with headless Dave's own expanding red wave.

Julia held Billy, the both of them horrified and speechless. Charm, held close by Betts, looked down at her father in disbelief, unable to comprehend what was before her eyes, in the way that shocking sights always took a few seconds to register.

Once again, smoke rose from the muzzle of the gun that

Officer Sherry continued to point at Ralph's corpse. The newly made detective was stupefied now, her face and mind both momentarily blank.

"*Daddy*?" Charm whispered.

"You demon," Betts said to Sherry. "You couldn't have shot him in the leg?"

"It was self-defense," Sherry said absently. Her hands were shaking now, struggling to keep the gun trained on Ralph's corpse in case he rose from the dead and attacked with that bat again. "You're all witnesses. I'll take full responsibility for all of this, don't worry."

"Don't worry!?" Betts repeated, aghast. "You just murdered this girl's father right in front of her face!"

Officer Sherry stared down at Ralph's body. "It was self-defense," she reiterated, as if trying to convince herself as much as the rest of the room.

"Let me go," Charm said. Betts's arms fell away from around Charm, allowing the girl to fall to her knees beside her father.

Billy tried pulling his mother's arms down from around him, but Julia's arms would not budge. So he merely gazed down at Charm. "I didn't mean for this," he said. "I just wanted to tell the truth."

Charm cocked her head up at him with a waterfall of tears cascading down both sides of her face.

"We should call more police," Julia said. "Or maybe not. Fuck if I know anymore."

"Lord have mercy," Betts mumbled to herself. Wide, heavy teardrops ran down her own cheeks now. "What is wrong with this world we live in?"

"Actually," Julia said, "I think I should take my son home." Yet she stayed frozen, arms wrapped around her boy.

Holding her aching back with her left hand, Officer Sherry leaned up on one knee. She took a couple deep breaths and then pushed herself standing, the gun in her now bruised right hand pointed at the floor. The knees of her black pants were stained scarlet. She trembled, took a step forward, and bowed her head.

"I don't know what to say," Sherry said to Charm.

Charm slowly craned her head around. She had more tears, and they were mixed in with the splotches of blood on her face and ran down red, as though she were bleeding from the eyes. Kneeling beside her father's corpse, she merely stared back at Officer Sherry, weeping hard—almost as if for the first real time that night.

If Charm still had her senses about her, she would've claimed that she really had meant to save Billy from the beginning, regardless of how it looked—regardless of how involved she appeared to have been. She would've told Billy that she understood if he always doubted the part she had to play to save him. She would've understood because, like she'd told him the night before, sometimes the truth really was just too absurd to believe. Yet she should've just told the absurd truth right from the get-go, because telling lies was always worse. Lies ignited wild chains of events that could cascade into uncontrolled, random chaos. Lies destroyed people, got people killed. Sometimes bystanders. And she was so darn sorry for it all. That's what she would've said to Billy if she'd had her senses about her.

But she didn't have her senses about her, and Charm instead self-destructed in a raging inferno worthy of all the monster gods of the netherworld.

"You killed my dad!" she shouted at Officer Sherry before throwing her head to the ceiling and screaming at the top of her lungs, louder than anyone had raised their voice all night. "I'll kill you all!" Her roar bounded off the kitchen's walls, echoing inside the ears of everyone still left alive. She looked at Billy with a ferocious snarl. "I grant you mercy and this is how you repay me!? I—I masterminded everything! The whole thing was my creation! The cult, the murder plan, everything! Tildra wrote her journals on my orders! Maggie-Lynn bowed to *me*! And I snuffed them out! And you can't prove anything! I'm in shock! I can say what-ever I want!"

Charm indeed was in shock. Her infernal revelations were a lie—at least to Officer Sherry. No way could Charm have planned anything being in the city all summer and having not yet met the new girl Tildra. To Sherry, Charm was surely just traumatized and stinging back—coherently or incoherently—in the only way she immediately could. With her words. Perhaps her mind had broken.

Betts was also visibly shocked, overwhelmed by the horror of what she was hearing from the mouth of her grand-goddaughter. She went pale real fast and leaned on her side with a hand on her hip, as if in great pain—as if she *believed* Charm's infernal revelations. "Oh, Lord," she mumbled. "Oh, no. Oh, Lord. Lord, oh, Lord."

"I was gonna kill you!" Charm blasted on, wide-eyed with rage and madness, death-staring Billy. "But then how would my infamy be born!?" She held up her palms in the air. "By letting you breathe and tell my legend, I make way for the fear of a coming scourge! The scourge of a thousand massacres! For the monster gods!"

Julia held Billy, the both of them staring down at Charm, totally astounded. Officer Sherry, meanwhile, found herself looking back down at the carnage she feared she'd caused, only half-listening to Charm's nonsensical rant, her mind suddenly more occupied by the two bodies drenching the floor in red.

"I've sent two to the netherworld already—and I'll send the rest of y'all to the gods as well!" Charm shouted, still going strong. "I, the reigning demon queen of the Sisterhood of Bloody—"

Charm abruptly went silent.

She looked over her shoulder.

Betts pulled the knife out of Charm's back and held it up, no doubt one of the blades on the kitchen floor that Ralph's flying corpse had knocked off the counter. Betts was on one knee behind Charm—one hand on the girl's shoulder, one dripping, bloody knife held up in the other.

"*Jesus Christ*," Julia said in a breathy exhale.

"You don't have the decency to wait 'til my life is over before throwing yours away!?" Betts bellowed. Her face caved in on itself, showing tortured agony, giant-sized teardrops falling down her visage. "After everything I've done for you and yours!?" She momentarily stared at her grand-godchild as though waiting for a response, an answer, squinting through her tears. Then she screamed on. "I should have known you for the evil you are the day you killed your mother!"

And here Julia gasped, mystified, having forgotten Betts's story at the beginning of the night, how Charm's mother had passed after childbirth.

Officer Sherry finally had her gun on Betts. "Put the knife down! Please!"

But Betts was mad. She brought the knife down all right, to stab Charm again.

Sherry pulled the trigger twice and hit Betts with two bullets in the gut, ripping the older woman's belly apart.

But not before Betts planted the knife in the center of Charm's back.

"Jesus fucking Christ!" Julia screeched. She managed to cover Billy's ears during the blasts this time.

Betts keeled over onto the floor, now holding her gaping bloody middle. Charm still sat up on her knees. She was reaching around herself with one twitching arm, trying to pull the knife from her back, but just couldn't quite reach.

"Okay," Officer Sherry said. "There it is, then." She looked at Julia. "Time to go."

"They need help!" Julia said. "We have to call—"

"Faster to radio." Sherry's face was cloud-white now. "Radio's in the car. Car's by the yard. Let's go."

Charm fell onto her side.

Julia gave Officer Sherry a fearful look from the corner of the room where she remained unmoved, her son wrapped in her arms as though the worst could still happen to him at any second. "Can you please put the gun away?" She asked.

Sherry's hands were shaking again, and it took her a few tries to fit her weapon into her holster. Her right hand was bruised purple. She sighed, then looked back up at Julia and asked with genuine concern, "Did I throw my fist up the horse's ass?"

"*What?*"

Sherry patted her gun with her purple hand, her eyes scared and desperate. "What I mean is, do you think they'll take this away from me? After it's all said and done? My badge too?"

Julia looked at Sherry as though the newly made detective were a total crackpot that put Maggie-Lynn, Tildra, and Charm all to shame.

"I didn't mean for—" Billy began to say to whatever remained of Charm, but his mother interrupted him.

"Let's go, William," she said, unknowingly calling him by his birth name, his arm still clutched tight in her grasp.

Julia, Billy, and Officer Sherry—completely covered in blood in the completely blood-covered kitchen—carefully tiptoed around the corpses of Detective Dave and Ralph Wilson and the bleeding bodies of Charm and Betts.

"I'm gonna go get help," Sherry said to Charm and Betts, glancing back and forth between the two. "Stay here."

Mother, son, and officer of the law left the kitchen and walked out of the house.

* * *

Minutes passed as Betts breathed heavily, laid up against the wall and holding her ruined gut, while Charm lay on her side, unmoving . . .

Until Charm Wilson did finally stir. She moved her head about, looking around, her back a bloody canvas with a knife in the center. Her eyes found Betts.

Betts stared back.

"*So this was my destiny,*" the family caretaker said to her grand-godchild. "*I have . . . long wondered . . .*" She nodded to herself. "*To end your line . . . To save this world from the scourge of a thousand massacres . . . Fair enough.*"

There was a long silence between them, Betts's heavy breathing the only sound.

Charm weakly asked her, "You think there's any way I can go to Heaven?"

Betts hacked up blood as, for the first and only time in this story, she laughed, a long and hard cackle, red spittle flying. "*You're gonna be chewed up, eaten, and worse where you're goin'.*"

Charm shook her head left to right. She was near-delirious but understood enough. "No, they're not gonna eat me."

"*Leave me be, spawn.*" Betts was huffing and puffing now. "*I need to . . . explain to your mother . . . why you're never gonna see her.*"

Betts closed her eyes.

Charm began crawling toward the sink.

It was a slow journey, inch by inch, splashing across the blood-soaked tile. The red flood seemed like it was a half-inch deep.

"Monsters won't eat me," she muttered back to Betts, whether or not her grand-godmother could hear her. "I'm worthy. I proved myself."

Charm reached the sink and crawled up it, eyes glazed, slowly hoisting herself standing with a wooden knife handle sticking out of her back.

Her arms shook on the counter as she held herself up.

She dripped blood. Much of it her own, much of it not.

She managed to turn on the water faucet and reach for the cupboard, opening it. She grabbed her fox glass, placed between the one with the rabbits on it and another etched with a pale gray horse.

For whatever reason, the thought of Tildra's "Magical Murder Mix" came into Charm's strained mind—that wicked, weirdly elegant classical music. It played in the background of her head as Charm imagined spectating herself from above—spectating her deeds of the night before as an outside observer—and not knowing what to believe regarding the true nature of her complicity, how guilty or innocent she was.

Was she really going to help kill Billy? Or was she trying to save him all along? Did her intentions change as the night changed?

Charm wondered what the gods perceived when they spectated the world. How much of what transpired in her realm could a higher observer decipher? Were they all-knowing?

She hoped not.

Shaking violently and struggling to keep herself up, she held her stance as long as she could and looked out the window. But the stars in the sky were not shining brightly. Their lights were going out. The storm clouds were coming in fast now, blocking out the Milky Way.

Glass in hand, Charm fell back, leaving behind more blood over the splattered counter and a red handprint on the cupboard door. The glass shattered against a table leg as her body hit the floor. Water flowed from the faucet into the sink. The dark storm clouds continued to gather outside the kitchen window, covering up the sky as rain began to fall. Finally, a giant bolt of purple lightning blasted down with a thunderous roar in the not-so-far-off distance.

ACKNOWLEDGMENTS

To the consummate professionals who aided me in the editing process—everyone from the beta readers to the editors I worked with—all your time, insight, and feedback is what enabled me to reach the final draft of this manuscript. I owe the completion of this book to all of you.

So to Roxann Acosta-Myers, Millie Godwin, Stormie Meyers, Simona Moroni, Amanda Nicole Ryan, and Jonathon Sterling, thanks for all the notes and much-needed advice. Thanks to Fiona, Jesse, and Stephanie at Quiethouse Editing for the valuable critiques. Thanks to Crystal Shelley for the wise words and thoughtful suggestions. Thanks to Alyssa Matesic for the eye-opening developmental edit. Thanks to Mehr Husain at Salt & Sage Books for the helpful sensitivity read. Thanks to Kim Stoker at The Artful Editor for the exquisite copy edit. Thanks to Trinica Sampson at Salt & Sage Books and Sherie ONeil at IWordyNerdy for the impeccable proofreads. Any mistakes in the published version of this book are my own.

I am grateful to MoorBooksDesign for the cover of this book, to Pauline Harris Editorial for looking over the blurb, to Savannah Gilmore for narrating the audiobook, and to Marina Baskakova, whose illustrations captured the spirit of VIOLENT NIGHTS and brought the story to visual life.

Thanks to Yoann Cifuentes, Jerrod Howard, Cynthia Monsivais, Josh Rosa, and Qadeer Stewart for reading this story back when it was a screenplay, and for providing the early feedback I needed—long before I decided to try turning it into a book.

My special thanks goes out to you, the reader, for taking the time to give this tale a chance. Much obliged.

Finally, I'm thankful for all my family and friends, without whose love and support I would never have been able to write this or any other story.

ABOUT THE AUTHOR

A lifelong dork, Ryan is a Southern California native who is proud to have been a pizza delivery driver for most of his adult years. In his free time, he enjoys watching TV and reading. VIOLENT NIGHTS is his first book.